John

Born in Surrey, England in 1908 into a poor family in which there were nine children, John Creasey grew up to be a true master story teller and international sensation. His more than 600 crime, mystery and thriller titles have now sold 80 million copies in 25 languages. These include many popular series such as *Gideon of Scotland Yard*, *The Toff*, *Dr Palfrey* and *The Baron*.

Creasy wrote under many pseudonyms, explaining that booksellers had complained he totally dominated the 'C' section in stores. They included:

> Gordon Ashe, M E Cooke, Norman Deane, Robert Caine Frazer, Patrick Gill, Michael Halliday, Charles Hogarth, Brian Hope, Colin Hughes, Kyle Hunt, Abel Mann, Peter Manton, J J Marric, Richard Martin, Rodney Mattheson, Anthony Morton and Jeremy York.

Never one to sit still, Creasey had a strong social conscience, and stood for Parliament several times, along with founding the One Party Alliance which promoted the idea of government by a coalition of the best minds from across the political spectrum.

He also founded the British Crime Writers' Association, which to this day celebrates outstanding crime writing. The Mystery Writers of America bestowed upon him the Edgar Award for best novel and then in 1969 the ultimate Grand Master Award. John Creasey's stories are as compelling today as ever.

THE BARON SERIES

Love For
The Baron

John Creasey

HOUSE OF
STRATUS

Copyright © 1979 John Creasey
© 2015 House of Stratus

All rights reserved. No part of this publication may be reproduced, stored in a retrieval system, or
transmitted, in any form, or by any means (electronic, mechanical, photocopying, recording, or
otherwise), without the prior permission of the publisher. Any person who does any unauthorised
act in relation to this publication may be liable to criminal prosecution and civil claims for
damages.

The right of John Creasey to be identified as the author of this work
has been asserted.

This edition published in 2015 by House of Stratus, an imprint of
Stratus Books Ltd., Lisandra House, Fore Street,
Looe, Cornwall, PL13 1AD, U.K.
www.houseofstratus.com

Typeset by House of Stratus.

A catalogue record for this book is available from the British Library
and the Library of Congress.

ISBN 07551-3596-2
EAN 978-07551-3596-7

This book is sold subject to the condition that it shall not be lent, resold, hired out, or otherwise
circulated without the publisher's express prior consent in any form of binding, or cover, other
than the original as herein published and without a similar condition being imposed on any
subsequent purchaser, or bona fide possessor.

This is a fictional work and all characters are drawn from the author's imagination.
Any resemblance or similarities to persons either living or dead are
entirely coincidental.

1

The Shadow

Wherever Mannering went, she followed him.

Whether he was by himself or with others, even when he was with Lorna his wife, she was liable to be just behind him; or alongside; or ahead, but never so far that there was much risk that she would lose him. She was conspicuous, if only because she always wore dark-lensed glasses. Because of these he had never really seen her face; and yet he did not think he would ever be able to forget her.

He could recognise her legs; her ankles; her hands; her arms; the shape of her neck and the way she wore her hair, clustered like auburn-coloured feathers. He knew the shape of her small nose, her full lips, her chin which was square and with a tiny cleft. He could recognise her ears. There were tiny blemishes, freckles and scars which would have betrayed her had she been one of a hundred women all dressed the same, with more or less the same figure.

She had a slender figure; unexaggerated; a slim waist; and whatever she wore her legs were always lovely, and the curves at her hips gentle.

She walked well.

He did not know whether her voice matched the rest of her, because he had never heard her speak.

Her shadowing had started over four weeks ago; or perhaps it would be more precise to say that he had first noticed her then, for there was no way of being sure that she had not been following him for a long time, without his noticing.

When he did notice her she was in Green Street, Chelsea, where he lived; he had forgotten some papers which he needed at the shop – Quinn's – where he was due in less than half-an-hour. So he stopped abruptly and swung round, and she cannoned into him. The only way to stop her from falling was to fling his arms round her in support; and for a moment he held her tightly. Then he let her go, and managed to say: "I am sorry."

She backed away, and with a murmured response hurried past him. He turned and watched her for a moment, noting her trim figure. She had on a suit of pale brown suede; he remembered the softness of it as his hands had brushed against it. Before she reached the corner he was on the move again. Stepping out of the elevator onto the landing at his top floor flat he was startled to see Lorna, his wife, with the missing file in her hand.

"Hello, darling," she said. "Don't bump into *me*!"

"Then you noticed that little incident?" Mannering said, smiling.

"Indeed I did. Every morning when you leave I stand at the window and watch you until you're out of sight."

"My!" he exclaimed. "What a lucky man I am!"

"Lucky?"

"Lucky that you don't follow me to the end of the street!"

Laughing, she stepped back and he pressed the ground floor button of the lift. He had a final glimpse of her, still laughing, as the lift started its descent. She was the most beautiful woman he knew, and even the few strands of grey in her nearly black hair did not affect that. Yet, he knew, that in repose she could look aloof, austere – some actually said 'sullen'. He had not known that she watched him, and felt an added tenderness and light-heartedness as he reached the street again and hurried to his car, parked halfway between the tall Regency house and King's Road, Chelsea, one of London's busiest thoroughfares.

He saw no sign of the girl into whom he had bumped; and

there was no longer any thought of her in his mind.

He was driving an Allard, a sleek car in metallic grey which undoubtedly suited him. There was room for his long legs, room for him to sit back in comfort, a tall lean man at whom women instinctively glanced; women in shops, in cars, walking, or standing in bus queues. Perhaps the most remarkable thing about John Mannering was his complete lack of self-consciousness. He was a perfect match for his wife, as handsome a man as she was a beautiful woman; and it did not occur to him that this attracted attention.

He had a little time, at traffic lights and traffic holdups, to ponder the papers in the briefcase on the seat by his side. They concerned an offer of a rare collection of antique jewellery, *objets d'art,* ancient coins and even some small items of early Egyptian, Roman and Etruscan pottery. The Collection had been gathered over sixty years or more by a man who had just died, and whose executors had asked him first to value and then to make an offer for the Collection. It said a great deal for his reputation that the executors, a bank and a lawyer of high repute, should ask him to do both.

So far as the valuation was concerned there was no problem. It would take him a week or more, fitted in with his everyday work. Any new major affair, during that time, would have to be handled by his manager and assistants. Moreover he had a standby assistant whose knowledge of antique jewellery was unrivalled and who would be overjoyed at the chance to come temporarily out of retirement in order to help. Buying the Collection was another matter: he guessed his valuation would be over a million pounds, which was more free capital than he had; and borrowing to buy always had its drawbacks; one had to sell quickly or the interest made deep inroads into profits.

There was no need to make an immediate decision – but the decision was not the only thing about the Collection which preoccupied him. It had been made, or so he was told, by a Mr. Ezra Peek who had lived in a large house near Basingstoke in Hampshire. There appeared to be no doubt about Peek's legal entitlement to the whole; none of their genuineness, but – how did one just 'pick up' such priceless treasures?

"What I'm asking myself," he said aloud as he turned into Hart Lane off Old Bond Street, "is whether he was a thief or a fence."

He glanced at the window of Quinn's as he passed towards a narrow turning and a parking place which he had at a new office block just beyond this tiny section of fifteenth and sixteenth-century London. But it was not the empty window of the narrow-fronted shop which attracted him; it was a reflection in it from the shop opposite and the woman standing outside that shop.

He felt quite sure that she was the woman with whom he had collided in Green Street.

As he passed she continued to stare into the window of an exclusive milliner's in which were five hats; tiny hats each on its own stand; as he reached the entrance to the parking places outside the towering office block of ferro-concrete the girl turned towards Bond Street and disappeared.

How could she have got ahead of him, he marvelled?

And *why* had she?

There were several possible answers to the second question and these passed through his mind as he parked the car and walked back to Quinn's. The most likely was that she wanted to talk to him but couldn't summon up the nerve. Another possibility was that she was a newspaper or magazine feature writer doing her homework on him. A third, simply, that she wanted to know where he was going and what he was doing; he had met attractive young women private inquiry agents before.

As he drew up outside the shop, Bill Bristow, manager of Quinn's, was placing an emerald tiara on a piece of black velvet, and although no sun shone directly into Hart Row the light seemed to sparkle on the emeralds giving them such beauty that Mannering held his breath and, momentarily, was oblivious of everything but the green fire. Bristow looked up, but Mannering did not really notice him. His breath came in short, sharp gasps and he felt his heart thumping, the blood pulsing through his veins.

It was like a seizure by some unknown, elemental force.

Throughout his life Mannering had felt moments such as these, part of the near mania for precious stones which possessed him. He was lucky, in that he could discipline the mania and, these days, even indulge himself in brief possession. It was an age since jewels had struck at him like this, driving all other thoughts but desire – *lust* – for them away.

Bristow withdrew and the drapes closed, his fingers disappeared and there was nothing to see but the velvet and the tiara, nothing of the shop beyond.

Slowly, Mannering went to the door.

This was as old as the beam across the fascia, the beams inside the shop across ceilings and walls. Some 'new' work had been put in after the first great fire of London, when a little group of houses here had been miraculously preserved, but most was truly old, hewn from the Forest of Epping when men felled trees with an axe and killed deer with arrows for their nightly meal.

The door opened, and Bristow stood aside; a compact man in a grey suit with a white gardenia in his left lapel; an ageless man who had seemed about fifty, all the twenty years and more that Mannering had known him. He had regular features and would have been called good-looking, but something prevented that: an absence of animation, no doubt the result of nearly thirty years of Scotland Yard's iron discipline. Once, he had regarded Mannering with deep suspicion; once, they had been virtually sworn enemies. Yet throughout those years there had been respect which had ripened into regard and become friendship. Bristow had been the Yard's expert on precious stones and *objets d'art;* his knowledge and experience were invaluable to Quinn's, with its worldwide reputation.

Together they walked along a narrow central aisle between small pieces of antique furniture, glass-fronted showcases, pictures on the panelled walls; it was as much a showplace and a museum as a shop. They turned to Mannering's office which was at the back, and never left unlocked. Opposite the door and on the other side of the aisle was a long Welsh dresser of beautifully carved dark oak, where small parcelling was done and some records were kept. In the panelled back were small holes, which appeared to be part of the carving. Through these could be seen every corner of the shop. Bristow's desk was here. So was one of the controls to a microphone and loudspeaker system which could pick up anything said outside the shop and be broadcast at a whisper or loudly to everyone inside. Mannering had lost count of how many attempts to break in and rob Quinn's had been foiled by that simple system.

He opened the door of his office, where his correspondence was tidily laid on a bow-shaped Queen Anne desk; the office was plainly furnished but for that, and a Regency chair some distance away from the desk. Bristow glanced up at a portrait of a Cavalier – the image of Mannering, at his gayest; and, indeed, it *was* Mannering, painted by Lorna years before.

"Close the door," Mannering said as he sat in his chair behind the desk. He was more himself, but still shaken as he went on: "That tiara hit me like a poleaxe."

"So that was it," Bristow said grimly. "You looked – well, you know how you looked. Do you know, John, I don't think I shall ever realise how much jewels mean to you."

"I don't suppose you will," Mannering said, "yet when I saw the tiara the other day it didn't affect me so much."

"Probably because then it was one of a Collection," remarked Bristow.

"Yes. Bill, I think we'll sell that tiara as soon as we can find a customer who will buy it. It's a crack to my dignity to let anything have so much power over me."

"There are alternatives," Bristow observed.

"You mean, I could buy it?"

"Yes, or else just keep it in the strong-room until it's lost its magnetism for you."

"Magnets never lose their effect," declared Mannering, and forced a laugh. "Let me think about it, Bill." He hitched his chair forward and placed a hand on the pile of twenty or thirty letters.

"Is there much here?"

"Another letter from Harcourt, Pace and Pace," answered Bristow.

He did not have to say any more to convey his meaning. Harcourt, Pace and Pace were the solicitors of Lincoln's Inn who were executors of the will of the late Ezra Peek, and who were so anxious to see the Peek Collection. Mannering singled the letter out and saw that it was brief and to the point.

Dear Mr. Mannering,
While reluctant to harass you we would be most grateful if you could inform us when we may expect the valuation of the Collection of jewellery and *objets d'art* now in the estate of the late Ezra Peek, Esquire. Further, we would be appreciative whether you think it practical to make an offer for the Collection as a whole or whether you would advise putting each item – or perhaps groups of similar items – up for auction.

Yours very truly,

There followed some squiggles which might have represented H. Pace and beneath these was typed the name of the firm.

Mannering put the letter aside and, looking up at Bristow inquiringly, said: "Why can they possibly be under pressure?"

"One of the legatees may have eager fingers."

"Yes," remarked Mannering, and after a pause he went on: "Do you have any friends in the Hampshire Police Force?"

"I'll try a call or two," promised Bristow.

His call elicited only the assurance that nothing was known about the dead man except a reputation for eccentricity, and the fact that he had travelled the world for years and his Collection was said to have been bought item by item, often in the lands of their origin. By that time Mannering had sent for Josh Larraby, once the manager of Quinn's, now a healthy octogenarian who lived in a small flat above the shop and was proud to be called the 'nightwatchman'. Larraby, who had shrivelled in recent years but still boasted a crop of curly, silver-grey hair and the most alert and intelligent blue eyes Mannering had ever seen, listened intently.

"I will be delighted to help with the valuation and classification, sir. I can imagine nothing I would like better."

"Then we'll get started," Mannering promised, and called from his office to Bristow: "I'll be locked in, Bill."

Then he crossed to the Regency chair and pressed a button beneath one of its arms. Immediately the chair began to move back of its own accord, and a wide hole appeared in the oak floor, revealing a flight of shallow steps. This was the only entrance to the strong-room, with its five different sections, in the first of which was the Peek Collection, its unique treasures already unpacked and set out on wide shelves.

Mannering and Larraby began to work, assessing, checking references in a Dealers' Handbook which was said to have a million entries, finding prices where prices were known on comparable pieces; and except for an hour's break at lunch-time they kept at it until after five o'clock. Larraby was still eager, though visibly tiring, while Mannering needed to spend an hour in the office on other business. It was nearly seven o'clock before he left Quinn's and walked through the gathering October dusk towards the car park.

As he opened the door of his car he saw a girl with dark glasses sitting at the wheel of an M.G. a few parking spaces away. He could not be positive, but felt almost sure she was the girl he had seen twice that morning.

2

To Tell Or Not To Tell

It was the same girl.

She followed him to Green Street, and drove past as he parked; the lift of her head, the small nose and the square chin, profile clear against the light from a street lamp, left Mannering in no doubt. She did not glance towards him. He found a parking place, preferring to leave the car on the street whenever there was any chance that he might want it again soon. He stood by it, peering towards the corner round which the M.G. had passed. He could see it vividly in his mind's eye, a shining red, as immaculate as the girl. He realised that this time she had not been wearing the pale, biscuit-coloured suit but something darker.

The car did not reappear.

No one appeared to be watching him from cars or houses nearby; there was no way of being sure of this, but one had a sense of being watched and he didn't have it now. He walked past the entrance to his house, which was one of three standing tall and dignified, survivors from the Nash period, whereas everything else in Green Street, contemporary or post-war, was either imitation Georgian or small apartments starkly and unashamedly new.

There was a haze of doubt in his mind and it did not entirely concern the girl. In fact he could not put it in form or words until he was halfway up in the lift, which smelt of a strong perfume used, he knew, by a recent tenant of one of the other flats. The doubt became a positive question: should he tell Lorna?

Aloud he asked: "Why on earth not?" and the doors slid open.

His mental picture of Lorna was so strong that he expected to find her on the landing, smiling, eager, as she had been that morning. The landing was empty. It served only their flat and the door was on the right. He stepped over the carpeted floor, hand in his pocket for his keys. His expectation of seeing his wife faded into puzzlement; there was no light shining through from the hall, the light which was always left on.

Was Lorna out?

If so, why hadn't she telephoned? Usually she did, so that he could have a chance to eat at his club or stay late at the office: it was a rare thing to come back in the evening without advance warning that she wouldn't be here.

She must have gone out and been delayed.

The more he thought of it as he selected the front door key the more he marvelled that a woman who had a career, especially such a brilliant career as hers, so often managed to be home when he was, allowed her own painting and all the business and social activity which went with it to interfere hardly at all with his.

Should he tell her about the second and third appearance of the girl?

What a question to ask!

He inserted his key in the lock, and pushed the door open a fraction – and on that instant knew there was something wrong. The strong perfume, faded since he had been in the lift, was very noticeable here in this dark hallway. Neither he nor Lorna knew the neighbour, but for the perfume to be so noticeable meant that she must have been here in the flat for some time – *or that she was in the hall at this moment.*

He hesitated – and then closed the door without going inside. Now his heart was beginning to race, partly from alarm and fear for Lorna, partly because of the situation. Was he being a fool?

Why should anyone—he cut the question off almost before he asked it. All his life he had been involved in dangerous affairs; all his life he had learned to notice the unusual. All his life his mind had worked quickly and incisively.

He believed someone was in his flat, waiting for him.

He believed Lorna was there, too, and since Lorna hadn't shouted out in warning then she was either gagged or shut in a room where she could not hear.

There was only one way of making sure.

True, he could go down to one of the other neighbours and telephone Bristow to come; or even telephone the police, but there was no certainty that his suspicions were right, and even if he *felt* that certainty as strongly as he had smelt the perfume, it wasn't enough to justify calling for help.

He slid his right hand into a small pocket in the lining of his jacket and drew out a cigarette lighter, or what looked like one; it was a miniature pistol and years ago he had adapted it to fire tear-gas pellets, in the place of bullets. When one lived dangerously, the bizarre and the melodramatic became the normal. He pressed the button of the lift and the car went down making a humming noise audible to anyone close to the door of his hall. Next he stepped very swiftly to the wall alongside the front door, on the side which would conceal him from anyone who opened the door an inch or two so as to peep outside.

He saw the heavy brass handle of the door turn, and held his breath. A moment later the door opened with great stealth, and he thought he heard heavy breathing: the breathing of someone with asthma or bronchitis. He was quite sure that a strong whiff of the neighbour's perfume stung his nostrils.

Then a woman's wheezy voice said: "He's gone."

"*Gone*? What on earth *for*?" asked a man whose voice was rough-edged but cultured.

"He must have noticed something."

"What the hell could he have noticed?" There was a pause before the man went on: "He must have forgotten something."

The woman said: "Hugo, I'm scared. I think we ought to go."

"And miss this chance? Don't be a fool!"

"Something's wrong, I tell you, and if we go now—"

"We'll go empty-handed and I didn't go to all the trouble we've gone to for nothing. Close that door and wait until he gets back."

"But Hugo—" The woman's voice rose in protest, and there was a scuffle of sound, as if the man was pulling the woman away from the door.

Mannering slipped the 'cigarette lighter' back into his pocket and stepped towards the door. The couple were too involved in their quarrel even to notice him, the woman clutching the door to keep it open, the man pushing her away with one hand and trying to slam the door with the other. Mannering sidled through, then gripped the man's wrist and twisted – it was the first intimation the other had had, and he gasped and turned his head. Mannering thrust his arm up behind him in a hammerlock as the woman backed away.

"If you struggle you'll break your arm," Mannering said mildly. He flicked on the hall light which was bright enough to show the woman's over-hennaed hair, her lavish make-up, false eyelashes and bright red lips. She backed towards a William and Mary slung leather chair, banged the back of her legs against it and collapsed; the leather seat groaned. "And if you don't answer this question quickly, *I'll* break your arm," Mannering went on. "Where is my wife?"

The woman's mouth opened and closed but no sound came.

The man said in a gravelly voice: "I locked her in a cupboard."

"Which cupboard?" Before the man could answer Mannering went on: "Lead me to it."

"Let—let me go."

"After you've unlocked the cupboard." Mannering gave the man a sharp push, deciding, after a quick glance, that the woman seemed to be in a state of collapse, and was unlikely to present any threat. The only cupboard large enough to hold Lorna was in the passage outside the bathroom, and to reach it they would have to leave the woman here. "Stay where you are," he ordered her tersely, "if you so much as move I'll have you both in jail within half-an-hour."

He pushed the man again.

Now his anxiety for Lorna was easing and his curiosity about the new neighbours was increasing. He had only seen the man once or twice in passing. From behind, he was thickset and broad-shouldered, had a reddish, fleshy neck and bristly greying hair, thinning into a small bald patch.

Mannering sensed a change in the man's movement, glanced down, realised he was going to back heel. Sharply, suddenly, he thrust the arm further up and the man cried out in anguish.

"Next time I'll break it," Mannering threatened.

They turned into the passage, and there was the bathroom door, ajar, a spare room door wide open, a loft ladder which disappeared into the attic, now Lorna's studio, and a cupboard next to the bathroom.

"Open it," Mannering ordered.

As the man fumbled for the key with his free hand fear for Lorna swept back over Mannering; he clenched his teeth as the door opened. On the instant he knew there was no need to worry but need for fierce anger, for Lorna had been gagged with a scarf pulled tightly round her mouth and knotted at the back of her head. Her wrists were tied together and tied in turn to a waterpipe which ran from floor to ceiling.

Mannering dropped the man's arm, pulled him round and struck him, once beneath the jaw, once in the *solar plexus*. Then, shifting his collapsed body out of the doorway, Mannering turned to Lorna, drawing her close to him.

He was acutely aware of her, and could feel her trembling.

He plucked at the knot and soon had it loose; he drew it away gently, seeing with relief that the marks at the corners of her lips were not too deeply embedded. Her incarceration, then, had not been for long. He cut the cord at her wrists and then supported her away from the cupboard, her movements stiff and wavering. He took her into the hallway, where the woman still sat in exactly the same position in which he had left her, the only difference now being that her mouth was closed and the breath whistled through her nostrils.

Gently, Mannering led Lorna into the kitchen, where there was a comfortable armchair. He fetched salve from the bathroom, poured out a weak whisky and soda and held the glass as she sipped, coughed, sipped again and then pushed the glass away.

"Thank God you're all right," she said huskily.

"Thank God I'm all right?"

"I didn't know what they were going to do to you."

"I have a feeling one or the other of them will soon talk," Mannering said. He kissed her forehead. "All right here for a few moments?"

"Of course."

He touched her cheek with his forefinger and went out, thinking: she is, she really is, the most remarkable woman. He stood in the passage outside the bathroom, looking down at the man, who was beginning to stir. There was no sign of feigning; it was more than probable that all the light had been knocked out of him.

Now the problem was what to do.

The obvious thing was to send for the police, but before he did that he wanted to know what the pair had come for, and the woman would undoubtedly talk more freely. So he bent down, straightened the man out, and dragged him along the floor into the hall. The woman cried: "Don't hurt him!"

Mannering dragged her husband into a room where the door stood wide open; this was a study, library, and general purpose room. Along one wall was an oak settle, carved by master craftsmen at least four centuries before. There was an arm at each end, and he used the scarf with which Lorna had been gagged to tie the man's wrist to one of them. Mannering ran through his pockets – and in the hip pocket on the right hand side he found a small, flat, automatic pistol.

He looked at this and then at the man, murmuring: "Well, well," then moved to a telephone and dialled Bill Bristow's home number. Bristow's wife answered. "I'm sorry it's so close to dinner time, Mrs. Bristow, but could Bill come to my flat at once?" he asked apologetically.

The answer came promptly. "I'm sure he will. And we've finished supper anyway, so there's no need to worry."

Mannering rang oil, and went to the hall, where the woman was now standing up, but obviously as frightened as ever. She put out a hand diffidently.

"Don't—please don't send for the police."

"Why were you here?" demanded Mannering. He was aware of Lorna at the kitchen doorway, standing, he noticed with relief, without support. She did not interrupt, and the other woman didn't seem to notice her.

"My—my husband thought—thought you always kept a lot of jewels here, so he—he—" She hesitated for a long time but Mannering did nothing to help her and Lorna did not move. At last, the other woman went on: "He wouldn't have hurt anyone, not really hurt, he—"

"What does he do for a living?" demanded Mannering.

"He—he's a commission agent, he does anything. If you'll let us go I swear we won't do anything like this again. I *swear* it."

"Why did you move in downstairs? Did your husband think it would be a good jumping off ground for trying to rob me?"

"He—he—he – oh, my goodness, oh God help me, yes, that's the truth, he—he lost a lot of money lately, he's not a bad man really, he—"

Bristow looked down at Mannering's prisoner and said without the slightest hesitation: "His name is Hugo Carter. He has a record as long as your arm, and he'll steal anything he can lay his hands on. Why his wife stays with him no one will ever know – she's a prison-widow most of the time." He looked up at Mannering and went on: "You weren't thinking of letting him go, were you?"

"No," Mannering said slowly. "All I want to be sure of is, whether he came to steal for himself, or whether he's working for someone else."

"He's always been a loner and I don't believe he'll ever change.

Any special reason for asking?"

Again Mannering said: "No." But it was not strictly true. He had wondered fleetingly whether these two people could have anything to do with the girl with the dark glasses. He did not want to suggest it now, with Lorna present: it might only alarm her unnecessarily and she had had more than enough alarm for one day. "Will you call the Division, Bill?"

Bristow nodded, and sprang to the telephone.

As he called the police, Hugo Carter's wife began to cry, quietly, helplessly, while Mannering went to the kitchen with Lorna, had a stronger whisky and soda than he had given her, feeling a tremendous relief that she had escaped so lightly.

There wasn't really the slightest reason why he should not tell her about the girl with the dark glasses.

But he didn't.

3

True Value

John Mannering sat at his desk at Quinn's, a month to the day after the attempted robbery; a month to the day after he had first seen the girl with the dark glasses; a month to the day after he had told Messrs. Harcourt, Pace and Pace that it would be five weeks before he could complete the valuation of the Peek Collection; and a month to the day after the emerald tiara had so affected him.

In that month the Peek Collection had become almost an obsession, it was so varied in kind, in origin, in beauty. The girl with the dark glasses had become almost a part of existence. For a reason he could not fully understand he pretended never to notice her; and in all of that time she had made no attempt to speak, write or contact him in any way. She was simply liable to be anywhere he happened to be. It was almost uncanny, for she seemed able to anticipate his movements and be at places ahead of him when he had gone there at very short notice.

But a pattern emerged, slowly.

She appeared only at places where he frequented; and so, where he was likely to be. Several times he changed his first choice of a restaurant, when lunching with a customer or a friend, at the last moment, taking them to a place with which he was unfamiliar. The girl was never at any of these. By now he had seen her in many different outfits, but never without dark glasses. Some things had become clearly apparent: all her clothes were of excellent quality and cut, implying that she was at least wealthy enough to afford good, expensive clothes. She never changed her hair style, however.

She wore little jewellery; a brooch now and again, or a simple necklace, all of which he judged to be of high quality.

And she wore no rings.

On this day – four weeks after their first meeting – he had seen her again when he had parked his car. Unaccountably he had not been able to forget her, despite Larraby's glowing face as he had said triumphantly: "This should be our very last day on the Peek Collection, sir."

"Yes, Josh, with luck. We have to check the typewritten valuation sheets. Otherwise—"

"I *have* checked them, sir."

"You mean you stayed up all night?"

"Not actually. I was up rather early this morning, sir – excited, I do believe. And I have also made a total valuation."

"Keep it to yourself until I've totalled everything too," Mannering said. "If we tally we won't need an accountant to check."

"I will indeed, sir!"

Larraby went out, leaving on Mannering's desk a large pile of typewritten reports, or valuation sheets: there were nineteen in all, divided into categories, such as: Gold: Silver: Porcelain: Ivory: Precious Stones: Semi-Precious Stones: Carvings: Paintings: Engravings: Enamelled Work. Alongside each entry was the country of origin, the known or estimated date of its first appearance and a short two or three line description. One entry read:

Ivory carving, Buddha, seven inches tall, six inches at base, darkened, ascribed to Wun Ching, Tapu, Ming Dynasty. Comparable carving sold at Christies, London, in 1954 for £10,525. Today's estimated value: £20,000.

Mannering buried himself in the task of adding up the figures; a computer or a machine could have done this in a tenth of the time, but he preferred to read each piece himself, then check his own and Larraby's assessment of value; there was much more to them both than a row of figures or a total, but when finally he made the final figure he sat back, amazed, almost appalled at his first error of judgment. He had guessed about one million pounds. The total was three million, four hundred and twenty-three thousand, one hundred pounds. He pushed his chair further back, and studied his own figures, then closed his eyes for a moment as if he could not believe what he had read.

When he opened them again the top sheet seemed to have a shadowy picture on it: of a young woman, wearing dark glasses. He sat absolutely rigid for several minutes, then, at long last, he stretched out a hand and pressed the button which would ring a bell in Larraby's apartment. The old man tapped at the door so quickly that he must have been waiting at the top of the old oak staircase.

He carried a slip of paper, and handed it to Mannering. It read: £3,423,100

His expression must have told Larraby what had happened, and delight showed in the old man's eyes. Mannering handed him the sheet on which he had made his tally, and said lightly but with underlying seriousness: "I mustn't make any more guesses, Josh."

"I don't see that it matters provided you check before you put on a price tag," Larraby said reassuringly. He took an old-fashioned gold hunter watch from his waistcoat pocket and ran his finger over the surface. "Will you call the solicitors before or after lunch, sir?"

"After, I think," answered Mannering. "And I think you should take a few days' holiday out of London, the weather's wonderful for the end of November."

"I may go down to Sussex and see my sister," Larraby said, "but I would very much like to hear the solicitors' reaction to this news soon."

"And so you shall," Mannering promised.

Larraby went out, and Mannering put all the relevant figures and reports into a steel drawer behind the desk, and locked it. Bristow was out, looking at some goods due to be auctioned at a private house in Ealing, but three of the young assistants at Quinn's were in the shop. All of these were comparatively new; Quinn's was a training ground for young men who subsequently went on to other, larger dealers as managers, or else opened their own shops. Bristow had once remarked drily that to become a member on the staff at Quinn's these days a young man had to be screened as thoroughly as for the Secret Service.

Yet Larraby had once been in prison, because he had not been able to control his love, his passion for precious stones.

Mannering went into the street and looked up and down – simply for a glimpse of the woman in dark glasses. He did not see her and there was no doubt at all about his pang of disappointment. Why was she so much on his mind this morning?

When was he going to stop playing the fool and find out who she was and why she was haunting him?

Haunting.

It was almost like being shadowed by a ghost!

He laughed at his own folly, partly for reassurance, and then turned and looked at the window of Quinn's.

There, solitary against black velvet, was the emerald tiara.

Its beauty seemed to blind him and the scintillas of light flashing from the jewels seemed to fasten like fibres about his heart.

The tiara had not been there when he had reached Quinn's that morning; why had Bristow placed it in the window since? Bristow never did anything without a purpose, but what purpose could he possibly have had over this? Mannering moved away from the window, heart still thumping, astonished at his own reaction; it was as if the emeralds in that single headpiece had a hypnotic effect on him. He glanced at it out of the corner of his eye as he paused, set his teeth and strode to Bond Street. He turned into it blindly although dozens of people were about – and one of them was the girl with the dark glasses.

She was coming – she appeared to have been coming – from the other direction, and was walking quickly. She dodged to one side, he to the same side; for a moment they stood still, facing each other. Then the girl moved swiftly to the kerb, stepped into the roadway and walked past.

"Who—" Mannering began.

People surged backwards and forwards. There was a policeman whom he knew slightly, a newspaperman who had interviewed him more than once. Mannering nodded, smiled, strode on. Now his heart was thumping for another reason: the girl.

What the devil was the matter with him?

Girl?

He had never seen her so close before; or at least never had so much time in which to scrutinise her: all of twenty seconds, enough to know what she looked like – that she was not a 'girl' but a mature woman, lines at her mouth and the corners of her eyes proved that. Not a host of them, not deep, but no young woman in her early twenties would have them. Thirty? Perhaps, thirty-five.

He crossed Bond Street near Savile Row, passed the police station and saw two detectives in plainclothes entering. Both recognised him, both spoke.

"Mr. Mannering."

"Good morning, sir."

"Good morning."

Mannering's smile was quick and bright; he hoped it was not as mechanical as he felt it to be. Two or three narrow streets along was a pub, the Golden Bough, where he came occasionally when on his own and did not want to talk shop or pleasantries with anyone. The food here was always fresh and good, and went well with a light ale. What he needed was not beer but a hard drink. Nonsense! He ordered the beer, served always in thick glass tankards, and helped himself to a Scotch egg, paid, and moved across to a corner where there was a high bench. He drank half the beer, and cut the egg; then looked over the partition.

Standing at the other bar was the woman with dark glasses.

She wore a suit of olive green tweed, or some loosely woven material with a gold thread. A light, just above her, seemed to put flecks of the same gold in the darker shade of her hair. She was looking straight at him, holding a small tankard in one hand, a sandwich in the other. He thought 'looking straight at him' but could not be sure because of the glasses; he knew only that her face was turned towards him.

He must speak to her.

He turned, but his path was blocked by a group of men who had come to share the counter; young, boisterous, taking up a lot of room. He passed behind them, encountering a man and a girl, and then a couple of stoutish women. The pub, which had seemed empty, was now crowded, a babel of talk and laughter. Mannering tried, unsuccessfully, to squeeze between a man balancing three tankards on an enormous palm and another who carried four short drinks. The door continually opened and closed, but he reached the end of the dividing partition at last, and sought everywhere for the girl – or woman.

She wasn't there.

He felt frustrated, furious.

But what did it matter? Why should he feel so angry or so involved? Why did the beer suddenly taste flat and the Scotch egg dry? He made himself finish them both, and then pushed his way out, using a side entrance to a lane which led to Berkeley Square. A taxi slowed down but he ignored it. A woman came towards him, about the same size and figure as the girl, with much the same poise and carriage but she wore no dark glasses. Could this possibly be her? Hope flared, his heart raced, only to slacken as they drew level. This was a much older woman who had once been beautiful in a severe way but was now showing her age. She glanced at Mannering and away. He walked round the square, briskly, baffled by his own reactions yet not attempting to pretend they were other than they were.

What the devil was the matter with him?

Why was she so often close to him and why did she always disappear before he really had a chance to speak to her?

Suddenly, a realisation came upon him, so obvious that it was astounding that he had never actually formulated the words or the decision before. It was very simple. *He must find out who she was.* The time had come when he could not keep the secret to himself. Now that he considered, he marvelled that he had hugged it to himself for so long.

He walked back to Bond Street and Hart Row and this time approached Quinn's prepared to see the emerald tiara and determined that he would control his emotions about the piece, but as he drew nearer his heart began to race again although not for the same reason. He was on the other side of the road and should be able to see the emeralds by now but he could not. Instead of the green fire there was a single Chinese vase, eighteen inches or so high, gracefully shaped, and of a pale, azure blue colour which seemed like a surrounding mist, almost a ghostly ectoplasm. It was unique and as valuable as the tiara but it was not the jewelled headpiece. He crossed Hart Row and saw Bristow and two of the assistants standing together near the front of the shop, and he judged that Bristow was excited, and had touched the others with the same spirit. As Mannering opened the door they all turned towards him, and Bristow – punctilious when the younger staff were within earshot and used to saying 'sir' throughout his Scotland Yard career – called out: "You'll never guess what's happened, sir."

"I wish you'd put money on that," Mannering said drily. "The tiara has been sold."

"Sold, paid for and taken away," Bristow declared, elatedly, but Mannering sensed something forced in his manner and was not surprised when Bristow's whole demeanour changed as they went along the shop and turned behind the cover of the Welsh dresser. Before Mannering spoke, and on the instant that the office door closed, Bristow said: "I doubt if you can guess who bought it."

A dozen names of collectors whose especial love was emeralds sprang to Mannering's mind, but naming any one of these would simply be hit or miss; and Bristow's tone and expression suggested that it was not someone whose name he could hope to guess. So he said: "No, Bill. I've no idea."

"The woman who has been following you about for the past few weeks," Bristow answered, then seemed to steel himself to face Mannering's reaction; it was almost as if he expected anger to flare up.

And he was right.

4

Bristow's Discretion

Slowly mannering's anger died.

Dying, it made him realise the obvious: that any man so used to detective work as Bristow, must have known about the woman; he should not be even slightly surprised by that. Slowly, too, full realisation of what Bristow had said came to him. That particular woman had bought the emerald tiara in the space of an hour – less than an hour. She must have come here straight from the Golden Bough, had probably arrived here while he had been searching for her.

"How long ago?" he asked.

"Not more than half-an-hour."

"How did she pay?"

"By draft on Major's Bank."

Major was one of the few remaining private banks in England, and was widely used for international trading. Mannering's heart missed a beat, for she must have given her name and her credentials. Should he show Bristow how eager he was to know? Bristow was regarding him very levelly but kept silent. A muffled ringing sound betrayed the opening of the shop door, and it was a relief to look through one of the holes in the carving and to see the middle-aged couple who had come in. One of the assistants, dressed in a grey suit of impeccable cut, went forward.. The man spoke in a deep voice with a pronounced American accent.

Bostonian, Mannering thought, before the assistant could say more than 'good morning'.

"I am very interested in the vase. May I see it, please?"

"Most certainly, sir."

"It hasn't been there for more than twenty minutes," Bristow said, half-amused. "If we sell two things out of the window in an hour—"

"Come into my office, Bill," Mannering said. "Charles will come if he wants us." He unlocked the door and motioned to a chair in front of the desk and they sat down. He made himself smile but it was not easy. "How long have you known that I was being followed?"

"A little over three weeks," Bristow answered.

"Have you any idea why?"

"Not the foggiest," Bristow assured him. "But—" He broke off.

"Go on, Bill."

"It puzzled me," Bristow said, "mostly because you were obviously aware of her and yet did nothing about it. So I assumed you knew who she was."

Very slowly, Mannering shook his head and echoed Bristow's: "Not the foggiest."

Bristow actually opened his mouth in astonishment, gulped, and sat more upright in his chair. It seemed a long time before he said in a rather strained voice:

"You seriously mean you've been shadowed for over three weeks by a woman you don't know, and haven't tried to find out who she is?"

"Four weeks and two days," Mannering replied flatly. "Since the day of the attempt to rob me at the flat."

"Good God!"

"I know," Mannering said. "It baffles me, too."

"You don't even know her name?"

"I know absolutely nothing about her except how she dresses and how she walks, and how she turns up at places where I don't expect her. Do you know, Bill, I have never heard her speak? What is her voice like?"

Bristow, gulping again, replied: "She has a slight European intonation but is very fluent. The draft was on New York, and when I telephoned Major's they cleared it without a moment's hesitation. She has credit up to a million pounds and a letter signed by the Chairman himself."

With an obvious effort Mannering asked: "What is her name?"

"The name she gave was White."

"You mean you don't think that is her real name?"

"Could be," Bristow answered dryly.

"What did Major's call her?"

"Madam White."

"*Madam?*"

"Yes – with the English pronunciation."

Mannering pushed his chair back so that his head touched the wall beneath the portrait, and was silent for what must have been two or even three minutes. Bristow continued to look at him levelly, and something in the ex-policeman's manner reminded Mannering of the days when Bristow had sat in that very chair, questioning him as a detective from Scotland Yard and obviously doubting the truth of what he was saying. Now there was less doubt than puzzlement in Bristow's manner.

"Why didn't you ask me what it was all about?"

Bristow raised his hands in a helpless gesture.

"It was your private business."

"You thought I knew her?"

"Yes," Bristow admitted simply, and Mannering watched from narrowed eyes, puzzled for a few seconds and then suddenly and overwhelmingly aware of what had been going on in Bristow's mind.

"You mean you thought it was an *affaire*? Oh, William, William!"

"I didn't know what to think, except that as you said nothing you must have had a good reason. I wondered if there *had* been a romantic interlude which you wanted to forget, but she—" He broke off.

"Well, go on," Mannering said impatiently. "You thought I was being haunted by an ex-mistress, is that it?"

"I thought that *might* be the explanation," Bristow told him.

"Glad it isn't?" asked Mannering.

To his surprise Bristow didn't immediately answer, when he would have expected him to answer emphatically: "Very glad," or something as positive. For no man knew or liked Lorna more than Bristow. They sat in silence again until Bristow actually began to form a word, but before it was uttered a low-pitched buzzing sound came from one of two telephones on Mannering's desk – the one from the shop. He lifted the receiver while still looking at Bristow, his lips set in a taut smile.

"Yes?"

"Mr. Mannering, I have a Mr. and Mrs. Wilson Waddington in the shop, and Mr. Waddington is extremely interested in the Ming vase which was in the window. He has made a close examination and would like to make an offer. I thought you would prefer to deal with the matter personally."

"Quite right, Charles," Mannering said at once. "I'll come and see them." He put the receiver down slowly and then pursed his lips before saying to Bristow: "Bill, will you call Harcourt, Pace and Pace and tell them I have the Peek Collection valuation ready – would they like to come here and see it this afternoon, or shall I take it to them?" He turned Larraby's note £3,423,100 round so that Bristow could see it, and the size of the figure obviously startled Bristow and took his mind off the girl in dark glasses.

"I'll call them at once," he promised as Mannering got up from his chair and went to the door.

Inside the shop it was another world; darker except where spotlights shone on special *objets,* or paintings had lights over them, and one or two places with tables on which customers could examine any small item in which they were particularly interested. On the right hand side of the shop Wilson Waddington was bending over the vase, and on the other side of the table his wife looked on with a similar expression. They were like worshippers at a shrine, the clearest indication that they loved beauty, and were not collectors simply for the sake of possession.

Mannering waited by them, Charles by his side, until at last Waddington straightened up. He had a round, pinkish face; boyish. But there was nothing boyish in his voice or the expression of his slate-grey eyes.

"Mr. Mannering," said Charles, formally, "may I present Mr. and Mrs. Waddington." As they shook hands, Charles faded into a more shadowy part of the shop.

Mrs. Waddington was both taller and younger than her husband; and her smile was brighter and touched with a more general interest. In Waddington collector and buyer were now coming to the fore.

"Mr. Mannering, how much will you take for the vase?"

Mannering answered: "Seven thousand five hundred pounds, which is fifteen thousand dollars."

"Would that include a certificate of its origin?"

"It would include an opinion of its origin, history and value from the British Museum," Mannering answered.

"We are flying back to New York tomorrow morning," said Waddington. "What formalities do you need to guarantee payment?"

"The telephone number of your bank in New York," Mannering said.

"I live in Boston."

"I'm sorry, Boston."

"The number is . . ."

Ten minutes later, after a telephone call to their bank, the Waddingtons prepared to leave. They were staying at the Westbury, close by, and would come for the vase at ten o'clock the following morning.

"One thing," Mannering said as he opened the door for them. "What brought you to Quinn's?"

Waddington smiled.

"My wife brought me, under strong protest, to the milliner's across the street, Mr. Mannering. When we went in there was an emerald tiara in your window; when we came out, this vase." He moved to the vase and touched it gently with his forefinger, much as a lover might touch a woman's cheek.

"And the strange thing is they didn't have a hat I liked except the one in the window – and *that* was an absurd price!"

They were all laughing when they came out.

Mannering went slowly back to his office, and the door opened as he reached it. Bristow appeared, took one look at Mannering's face, and exclaimed: "They've bought it!"

"They're coming at ten tomorrow morning, to collect," Mannering said. "You're quite a mind-reader, Bill." Suddenly he laughed, and went on quickly: "But not about romance. What did Harcourt and Pace say?"

"I've an appointment at their office for you at half-past three," Bristow told him, and as Mannering nodded went on: "Will you take all the papers or just the summary?"

"I'll have Charles or one of the others go with the file – I'll take the summary and walk," Mannering said. "Who knows – I might be followed by a woman wearing an emerald tiara!" There was a slightly artificial note in his voice, a noticeable pause before he went on: "Putting the vase in the window was a miracle of timing." As they laughed at Mrs. Waddington and her hat, there was much more naturalness in each of them.

It would take Mannering at least half-an-hour to walk to Lincoln's Inn; he left at a quarter to three, stood outside the shop looking across at the milliner's, crossed, and studied the too-expensive hat. Even on the stand it was obviously right for Mrs. Waddington, expertly trimmed with dark mink. He went into the shop and a plain, graceful woman moved towards him.

"Why, Mr. Mannering! I don't often have this pleasure!"

"How very charming," Mannering said, and made a mental note to make sure this woman was invited to Lorna's next exhibition of paintings or some other social function. "Do you remember the American couple who—"

"Came straight to you after leaving me? Yes, I certainly do. Tell me, *did* they buy the vase in the window?"

"Yes."

"What a funny life it is," the woman answered. "A hat at a

hundred and ten guineas is too expensive, a vase – but that's none of my business!" The woman's face, plain but full of character, crinkled in amusement. Her name was Shapiro, Louise Shapiro, and she had been at this shop for as long as Mannering had been at Quinn's.

"It's very much your business. I would like to buy that hat at a hundred and ten guineas."

"For *her*?"

"Yes."

"You *must* have got a good price for the vase," declared Mrs. Shapiro. "But what a charming thought. Shall I send it across to you or to her hotel?"

"To the shop," Mannering said, beginning to edge towards the door. He had forgotten Louise Shapiro's almost mesmeric character: how hard it was to get away from her. "And I must—"

"I've only one regret," interrupted Mrs. Shapiro, laughing, "and that is that I won't see her expression when she opens the box. *Or* see her wearing the hat. When she stepped in I thought it might have been made for her. Do you know the moment you see them what your customers will buy?"

"Seldom," Mannering said. "Now I must—"

"And I don't suppose I'll ever see the woman who bought the tiara wearing it, either," went on Mrs. Shapiro. "Life is full of frustrations! I only wish—"

She broke off, for two women in expensive fur coats, obviously mother and daughter, came into the shop. Mannering made his escape with a pleasant enough 'goodbye' but as he went towards the end of Hart Row he felt dazed. The woman with the dark glasses *must* have been observed by others besides Bristow, of course; he simply had not given that a thought. But Mrs. Shapiro's sly remark made him think furiously.

What construction did *she* put on the strange affair?

He made his way by back streets across Soho and towards Holborn, walking fast, thinking about a dozen things but hardly at all about the business he was really on: taking the valuation to the executors of Ezra Peek. At five minutes to the time of his appointment he reached the open front door of one of the houses – now offices of solicitors and barristers as well as apartments – where Harcourt, Pace and Pace had the second and third floors. He walked up creaking wooden stairs past notices of companies fixed on walls and the backs of doors. This place must contain as many registered company offices as any in London. A girl sitting behind a glass partition at the entrance to Harcourt, Pace and Pace, recognised him at once.

"Mr. Harcourt is expecting you, Mr. Mannering. I'll tell him you're here." She turned to an old-fashioned push-and-pull plug telephone and announced briefly: "Mr. Mannering is here for Mr. Harcourt," and a moment later flashed Mannering a smile as she told him: "Mr. Harcourt's secretary will come for you at once. Please sit down."

There were hard wooden chairs in a small lobby lined with leather-covered law books which seemed as old as the building itself, bindings torn and discoloured, titles, once bold in gilt lettering, almost illegible. He had hardly sat down and picked up *The Times* from a table barely large enough for it and an ashtray when a middle-aged woman with snow-white hair came down a flight of narrow twisting steps.

"Mr. Mannering? . . . I am Mr. Harcourt's secretary. If you will be kind enough to come this way . . . Perhaps I should lead – it's always difficult to find the way in these old buildings. They're regular rabbit warrens . . . *Do* mind the fourth step, it gives a little."

They reached a wide passage with oak panelled walls and doors on either side. She paused at one of them on which the name Norman Harcourt appeared in gilt lettering, tapped, and entered.

Sitting at the far side of an imposing desk was the woman in dark glasses.

5

The Woman in Dark Glasses

Norman Harcourt, whom Mannering had met only twice and at his office, was a tall, lean, hook-nosed man with beautifully groomed grey hair and piercing eyes only partly hidden by *pince nez*. He was rising from his desk, hand already outstretched in welcome, when one of several telephones rang. Distracted, he said a little peevishly: "I distinctly told them to hold my calls."

"I'll go down and make sure they don't bother you," the secretary assured him, while Harcourt hesitated, then lifted the receiver, and said testily: "What is it?" He listened for a moment or two and then said: "Mr. Arthur will discuss the matter; on no account disturb me again until I tell you I am free." He replaced the receiver and then looked at Mannering. "What is it about a telephone which makes one answer it?" he demanded, good humour restored. "Mr. Mannering, how very good of you to come and how very nice to see you again. I don't think you have met Mrs. Peek, have you? Mrs. Lucille Peek."

The telephone interruption had given Mannering the few moments he needed to collect himself. He could not be sure about the woman but he felt certain that Harcourt had not noticed how taken aback he had been. Harcourt's introduction did little to restore his equilibrium.

Mrs. Peek . . . Mrs. Lucille Peek.

Not Mrs. Ezra Peek.

But then she would no longer be 'Mrs. Ezra' if she were widowed; there might be no more significance in the 'Lucille' than that. Mannering looked across and smiled at her grimly. What would she do if he claimed an earlier acquaintance, and simply told the truth?

He bowed. "No," he said. "Good afternoon, Mrs. Peek."

"Good afternoon, Mr. Mannering." There was the faintest of accents in her voice which fitted Bristow's description exactly. She did not rise from her chair, or move at all. She wore a dark green suit, well-cut and conservative.

"Mrs. Peek is the main beneficiary of the will," declared Harcourt, "and my partners agreed that there was no good reason why she should not be present this afternoon."

"No reason at all," Mannering murmured.

"Thank you, thank you." Had Harcourt been a little more garrulous he would have sounded fussy. As it was he stared at the briefcase which Mannering placed on the large square-topped desk at which they were both now sitting, with Lucille Peek at the end by the window. Now Mannering saw that this room was book-lined from floor to ceiling, the books on thick mahogany shelves. The desk and chairs were also of rich-coloured mahogany; the leather upholstery was black. "May I be very forthright and ask whether your original estimate—"

"Rather more a guess than an estimate."

"I stand corrected, your original guess, then, of not less than one million pounds in sterling, was right?"

"Yes," Mannering answered. "But rather more below the mark than above it."

The woman leaned forward a little in her chair.

"By very much?"

Mannering wished above everything else that the woman would take off her glasses so that he could see her expression when he uttered the figure. But she did not, and there was no point at all in delay, so he said: "By two million four hundred and twenty-three thousand and one hundred pounds."

Neither of the others spoke. Neither moved. Neither seemed to breathe. Mannering actually started to move his hand towards the briefcase so as to take out the summary of the valuation, but he stopped. This reaction was uncanny; he was quite sure there was something very strange going on.

Then, Lucille Peek put her hands to her face, and to her glasses; as if she were going to take them off. Mannering felt his breathing become tense and tight, and he looked at her, ignoring the man. She touched the arms of the glasses: she *was* going to take them off. He actually held his breath as she removed them slowly, as if anxious not to disarrange her hair.

"You mean the total valuation is *three* million four hundred and twenty-three thousand pounds?" Harcourt asked in a faint voice.

Mannering said: "Yes," but did not look away from the woman.

She was not young; but neither was she old.

She had eyes which were the colour of gold, or rich, rich honey; and they gave radiance, *life,* to the rest of her face, at the same time drawing attention from it. They were so clear; the colour was so pure. Her face – even discounting those eyes – was beautiful enough; but he had not been wrong about those lines.

She said: "That is a great deal of money."

"It is overwhelming," declared Harcourt. "Overwhelming. And my dear Mrs. Peek, as I have assured you in the past, there is no doubt of the accuracy of any figures Mr. Mannering gives. He might err a little on the side of caution – shall we say conservatism, Mr. Mannering – but you may have every confidence that the value of your late husband's Collection is not less than this very high figure. Precisely *how* much . . ."

Mannering opened his case and gave him two copies of the summary which showed the total value of each group opposite the listing of that group, and the grand total. Harcourt handed one copy to Lucille Peek, then attentively studied his own. At the foot of the summary was a single sentence above Mannering's signature:

In my considered opinion the above is the true value of the

goods and items listed above and on the relative schedules of categories at this date, November 28th, 197 . . .

He caught sight of her lowering the document and turned towards her. She showed little expression but there was fire in her eyes. Harcourt made a remark which Mannering did not quite catch and did not worry about. The woman's gaze held him as if by some invisible cord.

She asked: "And will you buy them, Mr. Mannering?"

"I cannot possibly raise so much money for what might have to be a long time – this Collection could never be sold in one piece."

"Will you make an offer, Mr. Mannering?"

Harcourt began: "My dear Mrs. Peek—" but broke off perhaps because of the intentness with which the others were regarding him.

"No," Mannering said. "I could not make a sensible offer for them."

"Do you know of anyone who would?"

Mannering hesitated before he answered, not because he had any doubt but because he did not want to sound glib or stubborn. He wondered why she was so anxious to make a quick sale even, it appeared, at a considerable loss: but that did not concern him.

"No," he answered, "I think the range and variety and the uneven quality would make that unlikely. A museum might conceivably be interested but museums seldom have all the funds they need, and are unlikely to spend so much at one time and from one seller. I could"—he hesitated, not really sure he should go on but urged to take the plunge even though his mind seemed full of warning cries—"try to find an interested buyer, an individual or a museum, but I doubt whether there would be quick results." He was strongly tempted to ask: "Why is there such urgency, Mrs. Peek?" but kept the impulse back. What they told him must be of their own free will. But the question stayed vividly in his mind.

"Mrs. Peek," said Harcourt, rubbing his right ear slowly, "I think we have asked everything we reasonably can of Mr. Mannering unless of course you wish to discuss family matters with him, and that is, naturally, entirely a matter for you to decide. Entirely."

"I don't agree with you," Lucille Peek declared. The faint accent made her voice seem almost gentle, when in fact, he suspected, there was the strength of steel behind it. "There is no need to discuss family matters if we simply ask Mr. Mannering if he will try to find a buyer for the Collection. Do you need confidences in order to accept such a commission, Mr. Mannering?"

"I wouldn't, ordinarily."

"Then will you try to find a buyer as quickly as possible?" After a slight pause he started to go on with a glance at Harcourt who was now moving his long, pale hands a little uncomfortably.

"My dear lady—" he attempted to stop her.

"This is simply a business matter," she swept on. "What commission would you charge on a sale, Mr. Mannering? Or alternatively, what fee would you expect before you started to look for a buyer?"

"My *dear* Mrs. Peek." Harcourt unlinked his fingers and rubbed the lobe of his ear again. "I simply cannot agree—"

"It is Mr. Mannering who has to agree," she broke in quietly.

"Unhappily, no," said Harcourt. He looked genuinely distressed. "At least not without a full knowledge of the facts. I simply would not permit him to handle such a task without being fully informed of the circumstances. And when it came to the point, neither would you. I am quite sure you would not—"

Mannering stood up, very slowly and deliberately, and said with his usual ease of manner: "I'm sure this is a matter you should discuss on your own. Mr. Harcourt, the other documents are on their way to you by special messenger, they may have arrived by now. Mrs. Peek, I am very glad we have met." He bowed and smiled drily, and thought: *could* she have bought that tiara? and reached the door. He had a feeling of disappointment, of being let down. Perhaps it was the fact that there was no longer any mystery about the identity of the woman with the dark glasses. Perhaps it was that she obviously wanted him to take on a commission which was either dangerous or illegal; why else should Harcourt behave as he had done?

Mannering opened the door and stepped into the carpeted passage. He half-hoped that Lucille Peek would call him back, but she did not. Harcourt's voice alone, baffled, rather peevish, faintly reached him: "Mr. Mannering, I do ask you . . ." as he made his way down the stairs: all of them creaked and two yielded half-an-inch or so under his weight. He negotiated them safely, however, and reached the reception office to see the girl at the switchboard turning in his direction.

"Mr. Mannering, Mr. Harcourt would be so glad if you could wait for a few moments, he feels sure the misunderstanding can be easily cleared up." So Harcourt had actually telephoned through to this girl about a 'misunderstanding'. Would it be churlish to refuse? He hesitated, and then said: "I didn't realise there had been any misunderstanding, but I will certainly wait."

As the girl passed back the message, Mannering turned to the waiting-room which was now brightly lit by fluorescent daylight strip giving an unnatural glow to the faded volumes on the shelves. At the far end was an elderly man; probably here to make a will or a settlement, Mannering thought idly.

He turned to *The Times*, found an obituary of a man who had often bought from and sold to Quinn's, glanced through advertisements for the big salerooms in London and the provinces, and then became absorbed in an article about an ill-fated group of mountaineers who had perished in an attempt to conquer one of the lesser known peaks in the Himalayas.

He became aware of movement, close by him; someone looked down for a moment and then sat down two or three chairs away from him. Out of the corner of his eye he saw the toe of a well-cut shoe, and knew that it was the woman with the dark glasses who was sitting there. He lowered his newspaper and folded it with slow deliberation; then asked pleasantly: "Are you waiting for Mr. Harcourt, too?"

"No," she answered. "I am waiting for you."

"I understood that Mr. Harcourt thought another word would be useful."

"He did," she said. "A word with me. He has osteoarthritis in his knee, I understand, and cannot get up and down stairs very comfortably. He asked me to give you his apologies." She paused as if expecting Mannering to make some comment but when he did not do so she went on, smiling faintly.

He realised that was the first time he had ever seen her smile. And the simple, unarguable fact was that it made his heart beat faster.

"Mr. Harcourt also persuaded me that if I desired your help I must tell you all the circumstances. Indeed he delivered an ultimatum, and told me that he would have the Collection brought away from your premises if I did not tell you immediately. And his firm *are* my executors."

"They are a very trustworthy firm," Mannering remarked.

"And also, very timid," she declared. "Perhaps not as trustworthy or respectable as you would think, either." She was speaking in a voice so low-pitched that there was no risk of the other couple overhearing. "They are aware that my husband was probably murdered but have not reported this to the police. Yet obviously they take the probability very seriously, for they will not permit you to help me unless you are aware, in the beginning, that there would be very much danger involved."

"And you are afraid that if you tell me about the danger, I will refuse to have anything more to do with the Collection or with you. Is that it, Mrs. Peek?"

"Yes," she answered simply.

6

Dinner for Two

She did not smile, yet Mannering had a feeling there was a hint of laughter in her voice. But it was hidden, far away, and he was – or thought he was – aware of something else in her. Not fear, but – hurt? How absurd! What on earth could have caused it? Not what was happening now, obviously, but perhaps what had happened in Harcourt's room. There she had behaved in a way which, when he looked back, carried the impression that she had been watchful and wary all the time, as hurt people often were. Now she looked at him directly and he could just make out the shape of her eyes, their golden brightness obscured. In one way she had been aggressive, in another she had been on the defensive.

What a strange interview it had been; particularly when she had so obviously wanted to ask him to work for her and Harcourt had been so obviously against it, and yet diffident about saying so.

These thoughts passed quickly through his mind and yet it seemed a long time before he spoke; and then it was with a question which seemed to have nothing to do with the present situation.

"Do you have to wear those dark glasses, Mrs. Peek?"

"I am used to wearing them, when I am out of doors."

"Do you wear them for disguise?" When she did not answer,

he went on: "Or to hide your expression?"

"Is it important?" she asked.

"To me, very important."

"Why?"

"I like to be able to judge the reaction of whoever I am with. I can't with you, while you wear those glasses."

She made no move to take them off, but a glimmer of genuine amusement crossed her face. He wondered what was passing through her mind. He wondered whether her husband really had been murdered, and whether Harcourt believed that to be true. He wondered why she was so anxious to dispose of the Collection. And he wondered what she would look like with the emerald tiara in her hair.

He *knew* what she would look like.

Superbly beautiful.

And he *knew* what he would feel: a tumultuous heart because of the stones and the life she would breathe into them. Their own life plus hers would be almost unbearable. Out of the blue, unbidden, there came a mental picture of a kind so startling that it was like a vision. Of this woman standing, naked, with the emeralds in her hair. Such visions could drive a man mad.

The smile at her lips faded. He could not be sure but he thought she was drawing her eyebrows together in a frown. Two voices seemed to cry out within him, one in warning: Have done with her, forget this madness! And the other saying: She needs your help; have you ever refused to give help where it was needed?

She stirred, and said quietly: "You are afraid, aren't you, Mr. Mannering?"

"No," he said. "Not afraid, certainly not afraid of danger if I should help you with the Collection, but – I am puzzled. And there is too much that I don't know. I would want to know everything before I worked with you."

"Everything?"

"Yes," he replied, "including the reason why you have followed me so often and for so long."

She said quietly: "That might be the most difficult of all the things I would have to tell you." She stood up, with such grace of movement that he could not fail to be affected by it.

Stay away from her, stay away from danger, a voice exhorted him.

It was not physical danger that he feared.

"Mr. Mannering," she said, "I need more time to think about this. And perhaps you also need more time." Was she reading his thoughts? "Will you come and dine with me this evening?"

No, say no, she is seducing you.

"I would like to," he said. "I'm not sure whether my wife has any plans that it would be difficult to cancel."

"How soon will you know?"

"By half-past five."

"Then I will telephone you at your office at a little after half-past five," she said, and suddenly, with a slight wave of her hand, she was gone. He heard her footsteps on the wooden stairs, receding, fading. There were voices, other footsteps, a bell ringing. The girl and the man he thought was her father had gone and he had not noticed either of them move. People passed to and fro, and must have been doing so all the time, but he had not noticed, he had been so utterly absorbed in Lucille Peek.

He stood up, glancing at an old-fashioned clock with a big round face and Roman numerals above the doorway. It was a quarter to five. How could so much have happened in an hour and a quarter – so much and yet so little?

Little? He laughed, but without amusement, the arrow of derision pointing at himself.

He went out. There was a middle-aged man at the reception window, manning the switchboard. He did not appear to notice Mannering as he passed down the stairs. There was no sign of Lucille Peek, but one of thirty or so cars parked beneath trees which were dark and leafless against the sky was a red M.G. There were hundreds of red M.Gs. about. A taxi turned in at the gates and deposited a passenger halfway along the row of houses. Mannering beckoned him and he drove up.

"Hart Row, Bond Street," he said as he got in.

It was a new taxi, and as taxis go, very comfortable. He sat with his legs outstretched, not so much thinking as reacting. The simple truth was, that the woman he now knew as Lucille Peek had had a disturbing effect on him from the moment he had turned to find her so close behind him in Green Street. Why *had* she followed him about?

Unless he decided to have dinner with her tonight, would he ever find out?

Did it matter whether he ever found out or not?

The truth was, he didn't know; Supposing at half-past five he simply told her he was sorry, he could not go, there was a family engagement to which his wife had committed him. He felt as nearly sure as he could that she would accept that; would assume that he really meant that he did not wish to accept her invitation and was using Lorna as an excuse. And along with that would go her acceptance that he wanted nothing more to do with her or the Peek Collection.

Quietly, he said to the empty cab: "But I do want to go. That's not the question: the question is, should I?"

He woke to his surroundings and saw that they were already in Bond Street. "The corner will do," he told the driver, and for a moment stood looking about him. She wasn't there – of course she wasn't there! He walked briskly along to Quinn's, and paused for a moment in admiration, for Bristow had placed on display a single miniature, which drew his eye as it must draw the eye of everyone who passed. Bristow had a rare and unexpected gift of window dressing.

He entered the shop, and was surprised to find at least seven prospective customers, many more than usually appeared at one time. Charles was dealing with two elderly men, the other assistants were also engaged with couples, Bristow was talking to a small, black-haired young man whom Mannering recognised only as Japanese. He went straight to his office; only Bristow appeared to notice him, flashing him a quick, searching look as he passed. Mannering unlocked the office door and went straight to the desk, seeing several notes placed for his attention.

The first read:

Wilson Waddington's credit is fully established.

The second read:

Mr. Norman Harcourt has called twice – will you call him back?

The third read:

Mr. Hiro Mitsu, youngest partner in Mitsu of Tokyo, is in the shop – if you don't come to see him I'll make a morning appointment.

The fourth read:

Lorna telephoned to say that she's been asked to go to an Arts Council meeting tonight and will be gone by six o'clock. Perhaps you will eat at your club.

All of these had "W.B.' initialled beneath them.

Lorna, then, wouldn't be in.

He could almost hear Lucille Peek's voice: "Will you come and dine with me this evening?" and his own answer, that he would have to make sure that his wife hadn't committed him to some other appointment. Now he had to decide simply on his own desires: he need not think that by dining with another woman he would be leaving Lorna to her own resources at home. Not, on a simple business occasion, that Lorna would have minded.

But was it to be a simple business occasion?

Mannering sat on a corner of his desk and dialled the number of Harcourt, Pace and Pace. It was now a quarter-past five and as the ringing sound went on and on he began to wonder whether the office was closed, but as he started to lower the receiver a girl answered breathlessly.

"Harcourt Pace."

"Mr. Mannering speaking. I—"

"Oh, Mr. Mannering, Mr. Harcourt's down on this floor now, he hoped you would call, please hold on."

Mannering studied the list of notes as he waited, telling himself that he should have gone to see Mitsu, for the Tokyo firm was one of the best antique dealers in the Far East. He leaned forward and pressed Bristow's buzzer: not Bristow but Josh Larraby opened the door.

"You did ring, Mr. Mannering, didn't you?"

"Yes. Ask Bill if he can keep Mr. Mitsu for a few minutes, I'll be out as soon as I've made this call." Larraby withdrew and the door clicked to as Harcourt came on the line. His voice was low-pitched and faintly conspiratorial.

"Mr. Mannering, how good of you to call. I was anxious to have a word with you, very anxious indeed." Another voice sounded, louder although obviously further away. "I am in a somewhat conspicuous place and do not wish what I say to be overheard, I do hope you can hear me."

"I can hear you," Mannering assured him.

"Good. Mr. Mannering, Ezra Peek was for many years a client, a most valued client of mine. Most valued. Mrs. Lucille Peek whom you met is his second wife, and the relations between his two sons and Mrs. Lucille Peek are somewhat strained. I speak with restraint, you understand. There is no doubt at all of the validity of the will. Proper provision was made for his children, substantial provision including his house in Ealing and considerable property in and near London as well as stocks and shares. I tell you this in absolute confidence, you understand. Absolute confidence."

On an open telephone, Mannering wondered: with a girl operator at the switchboard? But he said: "Of course," and waited for the other man to go on.

"Mrs. Lucille Peek was left an annuity, a reasonable and fairly substantial one for a new wife of only three years, together with the Collection which you have valued. At first no one raised any objection, or challenged this – none of the family had the remotest idea of the true value of the Collection. In fact it was not until you gave your—ah—shrewd guess of a million pounds that the legacy aroused any comment."

Harcourt paused, and Mannering filled the gap by saying: "I see."

But it did not fill the gap. Harcourt's breathing became more laboured, it was as if he were beginning to gasp for breath. A heart attack? Mannering wondered. A spasm of some kind? The hoarse breathing was very loud in his ear now and he found himself gripping the telephone so tightly that it hurt his fingers.

Next moment, the receiver at the other end went down.

It was not replaced briskly or sharply; there was a clattering sound, what might have been a shout, then a louder clatter before the line went dead. Mannering was so startled that he hardly knew what to do best. Then he put down the receiver sharply, waited long enough for the line to clear, picked it up and dialled the Harcourt, Pace and Pace number again. This time the ringing sound went on much longer than before, but he held on until there was a break in the ringing and a clerk's voice answered: "Harcourt, Pace and Pace."

"My name is Mannering. I was cut off from Mr. Ronald Harcourt a few moments ago. May I speak to him please?"

"I'm sorry, sir, but Mr. Ronald's had one of his attacks," the man said. "He's all right, he'll be round in a few minutes, but he'll be taken straight home and I should doubt if he will be in the office for two or three days. Can one of his partners help you?" Before Mannering could answer the man went on: "Will you call in the morning, sir? Or shall I have one of the partners call you?"

"I'll call," Mannering decided. "Thank you."

He replaced the receiver very slowly. In one way he was relieved, in another more concerned than ever because he did not know what Harcourt had wanted to say, but felt sure that it had to do with his dealing with Lucille and the Collection. He sat on the corner of his desk, hand still on the telephone, everything forgotten except this. There was a tap at the door and Bristow looked in, his lips parted to speak. Mannering's expression obviously stopped the words but his appearance shook Mannering out of himself, and he stood up from the desk.

"What is it, Bill?"

"Mitsu has to go," Bristow answered. "I thought you might just like to say hallo. But he'll be here at ten-thirty tomorrow, so—"

"I'll come," Mannering said, and went ahead as Bristow stood aside for him. Young Mitsu, who barely came up to Mannering's shoulder, had a complexion so perfect that it looked artificial, and his eyelashes and eyebrows were as jet black as his hair which was brushed straight back from his forehead.

"I'm very glad to see you." Mannering extended his hand.

"You are kind to interrupt important business for me," Mitsu gripped firmly enough as he bowed over Mannering's hand. Straightening up, he went on: "I bring you greetings from my father and his father." There was a marked American intonation in his voice.

"My greetings to them," Mannering said.

"You are so kind." Mitsu bowed again, more deeply this time. "And my thanks for finding precious time in which to see me tomorrow. I am sorry I have a social engagement at the house of the Ambassador for which I must not be late. You will forgive me?"

"Of course," Mannering said, and walked with the Japanese towards the door, which Charles hurried to open. As Mitsu went out a telephone bell rang and Mannering thought: Lucille. He did not hurry, did not betray his inner excitement, but continued to walk at the same even pace towards his office. He was halfway there when one of the assistants called: "It's for you, Mr. Mannering."

"I'll take it in my office," Mannering said; he did not know what Lucille would say or what he might have to say to her. He told himself that he had not even decided whether to go and see her tonight, although in fact he was lying to himself. He pushed the door to with one hand as he plucked up the receiver with the other, and said: "This is John Mannering."

A man's voice spoke, quickly, decisively: "Mannering," it said,

47

"if you have anything to do with that bitch Lucille Peek you'll be signing your own death warrant. Didn't anyone tell you she's already murdered two husbands, one of them Ezra Peek?"

7

Murderess?

For a split second Mannering was too taken aback to speak, but the man did not hang up; regaining his poise quickly, Mannering replied calmly: "Who is speaking?" his mind alert, his ears keyed to catch every nuance of tone and expression.

"Never mind who I am. I—"

"But I need to know who has my welfare so much at heart."

"Mannering," the man said, and his voice was now harsher in tone and touched with anger, "you may think it's funny now, but you won't think anything's funny for long if you get involved with her. You would be wise to accept the fact that she has had more men than a hundred normal women put together. She destroys lovers and she *kills* husbands."

The last words echoed and re-echoed in Mannering's mind. Before he could speak, the line went dead and there was nothing at all he could do but replace his receiver. A chiming clock, just outside the door, struck one: the half-hour. Lucille was to call soon. He went to the door to find Bristow approaching and the last customer apparently gone. Mannering schooled himself to look as normal as Bristow, although those words still echoed in his head. "She destroys lovers and she *kills* husbands."

"You're looking very pleased with yourself, Bill," Mannering remarked.

"I'm more than pleased, I'm excited," declared Bristow. "This has been the best day, saleswise, since I came to work for you, and that means in four years. Apart from the tiara and the vase, over thirty thousand pounds together, we have sold forty-one thousand pounds worth of stock. You'll have to start buying, John!"

"Forty-one thousand!" exclaimed Mannering.

"Two Watteaus at fifteen hundred each, the Genoese silver table, four thousand, the small Louis Quinze secretaire . . ." Bristow went through the list in his head – another of his rare capabilities; he remembered virtually everything that happened during the day. His last item was: "And that little gold and porcelain clock outside your room, seven hundred and fifty pounds. My God! You get your hands on some beautiful things, John!"

"Congratulations," Mannering murmured. "We should have a drink to celebrate. Have the others gone?"

"Yes, even old Josh has gone upstairs, he's been helping us out nearly all day." Bristow watched Mannering take a bottle of Scotch whisky and a syphon from a cupboard close at hand, and went on almost casually: "How did you get on at Harcourt, Pace and Pace?"

Mannering began to pour out, asking himself as he did so: how much shall I tell Bristow? He was almost sure that it had to be all or nothing – anything else would be unfair and frustrating. He gave Bristow a whisky and soda which he knew would be to the other's liking, added more soda to his own drink, and said: "Cheers. And congratulations."

"The customers came *here*."

"Your window drew them," declared Mannering, sipping and letting the drink go down slowly. "Bill, I am due to receive a telephone call from a Mrs. Lucille Peek, who has been trying very hard to persuade me to take the Peek Collection off her hands quickly, largely – I gather – because her husband's children by his first wife might challenge her right to it. She apparently wants to sell the Collection while it is legally hers, and then skip. The skipping part is a guess, the other a reasonable inference from what Harcourt told me." He drank again before going on: "And that is not all. The last telephone call I had was an anonymous well-wisher whose crucial accusation was that Mrs. Lucille Peek destroys her numerous lovers and kills her husbands."

He leaned back in his chair, studying Bristow's expression. It was worth studying, for it changed from interest to alarm, then on to incredulousness and finally to something not far removed from disbelief.

Mannering chuckled.

"The telephone call was obviously to find out whether, after this dire warning, I will go and dine with this Delilah *alias* Lucille tonight." He glanced at the telephone and suddenly realised that it must be a quarter to six; as suddenly, felt gripped by alarm – yes, *alarm* – lest she did not call again. He glanced away, his smile now set as he watched Bristow take a deep drink and then put his glass down.

"You'll be telling me next that she is the woman with dark glasses," he said.

"As a matter of fact," Mannering told him calmly, "she is."

"You're fooling."

"I am telling you the gospel truth," Mannering said, and smiled more naturally into Bristow's face, seeing stupefaction chase every other expression away. For a few seconds they remained in silence, Mannering leaning back in his chair and Bristow standing like a statue.

Then, the telephone bell rang.

Bristow started: Mannering started. The bell went on ringing, and Mannering put out his hand for it. It might not be her, of course, it might be the accuser again, or even a late caller for the office: it might be Lorna. Come to think of it she probably would call about now, as often as not he would answer a call at this hour with a light: "Hallo, darling!"

He put the receiver to his ear, and said: "This is John Mannering."

"This is Lucille Peek," Ezra Peek's widow said in a controlled voice. "I am a little later than I had expected. I am glad you are still in your office."

"I was beginning to wonder whether you had regretted your invitation."

"You mean you will come?" Excitement flared up in her voice.

"If you are prepared to meet the conditions – that you tell me everything, including your reason for following me so often."

"Yes," she replied without hesitation. "I have given the matter much thought and I will tell you even that. Will half-past seven be a convenient time for you?"

"Perfect," Mannering said.

"I shall expect you, then, at my apartment which is seventeen – one, seven, you understand – Northcote Square. It's in St. John's Wood, not far from the cricket ground. Thank you, Mr. Mannering. It will be a great relief to be able to tell some good person the truth."

She rang off, quietly. Mannering put his receiver down slowly, while looking at Bristow, who tossed off the rest of his drink, but shook his head when Mannering stretched out to refill his glass. He dropped into a chair with a faint shrug.

"So, while you've been valuing the Collection, she has been keeping an eye on you."

"Apparently. In between destroying lovers and killing husbands, of course."

Bristow asked: "How often has she been married?"

Mannering gave an amused chuckle.

"According to Harcourt, twice, but he may not know everything about her." Seriousness took over as he went on in a hard voice: "I surmise that Harcourt was about to divulge some part of it when he collapsed from a heart attack."

"A *heart* attack!" echoed Bristow.

"So a clerk at his office who answered my second call said." Mannering stood up and began to pace the room, speaking all the time. "Bill, there is so much that doesn't add up in this affair; so much which is peculiar and inconsistent that I think we're going to have our hands full. Before I decide how deeply to get involved I'd like to know as many facts as I can get from independent sources. Can you persuade your friends at the Yard to find out if there was any suspicion of murder when Ezra Peek died? Obviously there was no case, but sometimes the Yard has a feeling about foul play."

"Will do," promised Bristow.

"And can you get them to find out if Norman Harcourt is subject to heart attacks?" Mannering explained just what had happened while he had been on the telephone, and before Bristow could comment he added: "It was a very convenient time for a heart attack. It could have been faked. It could have been self-induced. It could have been because he was about to betray a client's confidence and simply found he couldn't. Or it could have been caused by someone else – by some shock such as a threat from someone nearby, or fear that he was being overheard. He was nervous about that in the beginning, I could only just hear what he said."

"I'm sure I can find someone who knows him or knows about him," answered Bristow. "Is there anything else?"

"I can't think of anything at the moment," Mannering said. "Isn't that enough to be going on with?"

After a long pause, Bristow said: "I'm not sure, John." He drew in a deep breath and spread his hands over his knees, palms downwards, while looking up at Mannering from beneath his brows. "John," he repeated, and hesitated, while Mannering sensed tension in him, sensed also that he was ill-at-ease, even acutely embarrassed – and that could only be because of what he was about to say: or at least wanted to say. He had only the vaguest idea of what it could be. "John!" Bristow blurted out. "We've known each other for a hell of a long time. I've known you and Lorna for more years than she would like to remember. Since long before you were married." He paused, and then went on roughly: "This might be the time to tell me to mind my own bloody business!" He almost glared.

"Perhaps," Mannering conceded. "It might also be the time when I would like someone to talk to. Let me quote Lucille Peek's last sentence on the telephone: 'It will be a great relief to be able to tell some good person the truth'."

JOHN CREASEY

Bristow said huskily: "I really believe you mean that. John, this—this woman in dark glasses *was* a complete stranger to you, wasn't she?"

"Absolutely."

"Yet the effect she had on you was – well, remarkable."

"I know. But don't ask me to explain it." Before Bristow could speak again he went on: "Yet perhaps there is something which would help to explain it. There was no *reason* in the way I felt about the tiara, yet it set me alight. There is no *reason* for the way I've reacted to a woman I hardly saw, a will o' the wisp, a—a shadow. But almost from the beginning I've been – fascinated."

"Have you told Lorna?" Bristow asked abruptly.

"No," Mannering said. "She saw her the first time we met. She was watching from the flat. 'Met' is hardly the word; I swung round and Lucille was just behind me." Mannering moved to the desk and poured out more whisky for them both; this time, Bristow did not refuse. "I simply don't know why, but I felt it was something I should keep to myself."

Bristow said bluntly: "I think you are quite right."

"*What?*" exclaimed Mannering.

"I mean it," Bristow said. "Whatever it is is something so inexplicable that even if you tried to explain to a third party, it's unlikely you'd get through. Trying to explain to Lorna, who is so emotionally involved could be – well, disastrous. If anything you said struck a wrong note and Lorna reacted badly – well, strongly – it would create a barrier between you that might be very hard to break down. It's none of my business, of course, but I do feel that whatever happens between you and Lucille Peek you ought to keep entirely to yourself. Do you know that you—?"

Bristow broke off, drank half of the whisky and soda and lowered his glass but did not go on, until Mannering said quietly: "Don't hold back now, Bill."

"Do you know what an incredibly faithful husband you've been? Has it ever occurred to you that staying as rigidly faithful as you have done, can put a strain on your nerves which, in the end, you'll take out on Lorna? It's unwise to go on playing the

54

saint unless you entirely feel that way, and I'm damned sure you shouldn't try. And what's more"—now Bristow wagged a finger, his doubts about talking gone completely—"*this* is why the woman in dark glasses intrigued you so much. You weren't responding to her, you couldn't because you didn't know her, but you had to respond to something. You—"

He broke off, staring into Mannering's set face, and stood up, saying in a groaning voice: "Now I've gone too far. I knew I would, I never was any good at meddling. I—"

"Stop it, Bill," said Mannering quietly. "I don't know how right you are but I do know it wouldn't surprise me if there was some truth in what you say. Shall we leave it for now – on one condition."

"What condition?"

"That if you want to re-open the subject, you go ahead and do it."

"I don't think there's a chance in a thousand of that," Bristow said. He drew out a handkerchief and wiped his forehead, an indication of the tension he had felt, the strain this confidential talk had been. "I've been trying to work myself up to saying something like it for days. John, you don't have to be rigidly faithful to Lorna to prove your loyalty to her. Did it ever occur to you that if you had a—a friend, a—oh, damnation, a *mistress,* you might be a bloody sight easier to live with than you are sometimes—"

He broke off. Mannering laughed. Suddenly they were both laughing. Soon, they locked the office and the shop, without disturbing Larraby who was up in his little flat, and walked along to their cars through a night already giving more than a hint of fog. They were at Mannering's car when Bristow said casually: "Mind you, I'm not saying this wealthy widow is right for you! Goodnight, John!"

He walked across the nearly deserted car park to his own car.

Mannering got into the Allard but did not start off immediately. Bristow's headlights showed that at ground level the mist was thicker, but this did not seem like a night which would develop into a heavy fog, though there was a raw cold which made him shiver. He switched on the lights and saw that it was later than he thought. There would be just time to dash back to his flat, change for dinner, and be on his way to Northcote Square by a quarter-past seven. He drove oil', through streets which were surprisingly empty of traffic, and was near Lord's Cricket Ground at a few minutes past the quarter. He had luck, too; two policemen were walking towards him, and drew close when he pulled in.

"Northcote Square, sir – you're nearly there. Take the second on the left and then the third on the right, and you'll come to a curved road. *That's* it." The policeman's hearty: "Pleasure, sir!" followed Mannering's thanks. In less than five minutes he was in Northcote Square. The houses, he saw, were all in three storeys, only eight or nine of them on the left-hand side.

The last was Number 17: the number showing clearly on the fanlight above the front door. There were several parking spaces by the kerb which surely meant that each house was divided into only three flats at the most. Along the street were several tall trees with thick trunks.

A moving shadow appeared to flicker behind one of them.

Mannering parked his car without difficulty and sat for a moment with the lights on but dipped. He did not get out immediately but waited until his eyes were accustomed to the dimly-lit street, and although he appeared to be looking at the doorway of Number 17 he was actually watching the trees and the evergreen shrubs beyond.

A man's figure, dark and shadowy, moved towards the car as Mannering opened the door to get out.

8

Attack – On Whom?

He stood by the side of the car, appearing to be looking at his wristwatch, but in reality on the alert for movement near Number 17. He saw none. He was sure no one had entered the porch, which had white pillars, one of which would have been shadowed. He closed the car door, humming to himself as he went towards the porch; he sounded like a happy man. On one side of the porch was a name board, and the middle of three names read:

Mrs. Lucille Peek . . . Flat 2 (Second Floor)

He pressed a bell-push opposite this and almost immediately a woman's voice sounded from a loudspeaker which must have been built into the door.

"Who is that, please?"

"John Mannering," Mannering answered clearly.

"So, you are very punctual. Push the door when you hear the buzzer." She gave him time to absorb these instructions and as a harsh buzzing sound ripped the air he pushed at the door, still on the alert for sounds and movement – and on the instant, they came.

He spun round.

Shooting out his right foot he kicked one man on the knee,

went forward and snatched at the other's outflung arm and pushed it up in a hammerlock as he had done to the man Carter. The man he kicked collapsed, the man he held groaned with pain. He dipped into his pocket for the little gas pistol and used it on both men, who began to gasp and splutter, their eyes streaming. He pressed the bell-push again and immediately the buzzer sounded. This time he opened the door and thrust the first man in, blocked the door open with one foot and pulled at the second man, who was choking hideously. The gas bit at his, Mannering's, nose and throat; these men who had received a full dose must be in agony.

At last he had them both inside a wide hall which had only a long narrow table and two upright chairs in it; warm-looking red carpet ran along the hall and up the stairs. On the right of the staircase was another door, obviously the entrance to the ground floor flat. No one came from it, evidently the gasping and groaning of the two men had not raised any alarm.

There was a sound from above, and Lucille Peek called: "Are you indoors, Mr. Mannering?"

"Yes," called Mannering, "but I need some help."

"*Help?*" she echoed, and suddenly she came into sight at the head of this flight of stairs. All he noticed was that she wore a green dress and dark shoes, and in order to see right along the hallway she was bending down. "But who are they?" she demanded. "What has happened?"

"I don't know," replied Mannering. "Either they were waiting to get in when you opened the door for me, and were after you, or someone warned them I was coming and wanted to keep me away. Who knew that I was coming, besides you?"

She was moving down the stairs now, with the rare grace he had already seen in her. She looked slim and youthful, and horrified. She did not answer him directly but said in a low-pitched voice:

"You must not send for the police, please. I know these men. They are from my husband's family, I do not wish to make trouble for them."

He could take her at her word. Or he could reject the appeal.

If he did, then all he had to do was send for the Divisional police and report the attack on him; no policeman would be surprised that he had turned the tables, no one would be surprised at his tiny gas pistol; he often carried valuable jewellery about with him and had to protect himself. If he did that, the police might simply believe it had been an attack on him, and that would be sufficient for a charge. They would be kept in a police cell overnight, and come up for a hearing at the police court next day. But if he let them go, without doing anything himself – and he could not, here – and without sending for the police, then who could he blame but himself for any dangerous act they might carry out in the future?

Both men were coughing and spluttering and their eyes were still watering but they were quieter than they had been, and appeared to be completely cowed; he doubted if there was any fight left in either of them, and he did not think they could hear what was being said.

"Never mind what happened before," he said, very firmly. "Go and telephone for the police, please. I will simply tell them they attacked me as I came in." When she hesitated he went on: "You and I can decide what to do later – while they're in a cell."

The light fell on her in such a way that it made her eyes look as if they were afire; and it put fire, also, into her hair. She hesitated for a moment and then turned and went upstairs. Mannering studied the men. Both were small, one dark and the other red-haired. The dark one was thin, the fair one over-plump. It was difficult to see exactly what their faces, still scarlet and puffy, would be like normally. He felt an overwhelming temptation to look through their pockets and actually moved forward to make a start, when there was a roar of a car engine outside, a slamming of doors and a thudding of footsteps. He stood up and went to the door, opening it to two policemen; a third man was at the wheel of a car which had a POLICE sign glowing on the roof. The first policeman was the man who had told him how to get to Northcote Square; the others were policemen he had seen at various times on the beat.

It took fifteen minutes to convince them who he was, what had happened and how he had bested his two assailants, and he thought at one time that they would take his gas pistol, but the older and more stolid of the two men said: "We'll check with Division when we've got these two back there, Mr. Mannering. You'll charge them with assault, I take it?"

"Most certainly I will."

"We may have to ask you to come round to the station and make the charge," the policeman went on, "but we'll see what we can find out about this pair first. Have you anything valuable in your possession tonight?"

"No. I was simply making a social call," Mannering said.

By then, the two prisoners were in the police car and a second car had arrived as escort. Everything was conducted in the hall and on the porch. The tenants of the downstairs flat were out, only a few people gathered to watch the police drive off with their handcuffed prisoners. For a few moments Mannering was alone on the porch, watching, feeling very strange. So often he had acted on his own; now twice in succession he had simply handed prisoners over to the police, without making any attempt to force information from them; even without going through their pockets, which would have been so easy while they had been blinded and choked by the gas.

He had set the catch on the front door so that it would not lock. Now he pushed the door open and went inside. The hallway struck pleasantly warm. As he went up the stairs he pictured Lucille Peek as she had pleaded with him to let the men go, remembering how she had accepted his refusal. Within minutes the police car had arrived, so at least she had not tried to waste even a moment.

What reception would he get, now?

There was a small landing and a door blocking off what had once been a passage. At the side was the simple numeral '2' – without a name, above a bell-push. He hesitated for only a moment before pressing the bell and almost immediately there was a flurry of footsteps and the door opened.

A strange woman! All anxiety was now transformed.

She looked radiant and carefree, and stretched out both hands in greeting and, when he took them, drew him inside. She was so much smaller than he, and as he looked down on her he felt his heart thumping beyond control. The door closed automatically behind them as she held onto his hands; he thought there were tears in her eyes and wondered, *can* she be pretending? Her accent was more noticeable than it had been before, as words suddenly spilled out of her.

"Thank you, thank you for coming back." She spoke as if from the depth of her heart. "I did not think you would, I thought you would think 'She is a wicked woman and I will have no more to do with her.'" She gave his hands a tighter squeeze, then let one go and turned and led him into a room on the right, a surprisingly large room furnished pleasantly but unremarkably with a mixture of French and English period furniture. The strains of Swan Lake came very softly from a record player.

"You come without a coat," she said, "you must be a very hardy man. Oh, I am so relieved you have come back. First – a little drink, but not to linger because already dinner is perhaps cooking too long, but it will be eatable, that I promise you." Why did her voice sound so attractive, why were her eyes spilling over as if with happiness? "What will you have, please?"

"A whisky and soda, if—"

"Only an Englishman can mix a whisky and soda to his liking, but please, not *too* strong. I have cooked a great delicacy for us!" She moved towards a cabinet where bottles and glasses stood.

"And what will you have?" Mannering asked.

"For me, nothing, thank you. I do not ever drink alcohol before a meal; it spoils the flavour of good food. It is a habit I learned from my father, you understand. But please do not let me prevent you—"

He raised his glass to her, said: "To beauty," which obviously delighted her, and then lowering his glass asked: "Why did you expect me to think that you are a wicked woman?"

"But is that not obvious?"

"Tell me, please."

"So," she said, spreading her hands. The poise she had always shown before, the studied calm she had assumed in Harcourt's office were gone completely; she seemed to be a different woman.

Younger; more beautiful; seductive.

"So," she repeated. "I ask you to come here. Two men attack you. No one else knows you are coming so who could tell these men but me? Is that not one thing you have already asked yourself?" she demanded.

"Yes," he answered.

"So!" Her eyes glowed. "You are indeed the honest one!"

"But I asked myself a question or two as well," went on Mannering. "For instance, why should you make it so obvious? Too obvious." She smiled in appreciation of his reasoning, as he went on: "Also – did they come to attack me, or to attack you? Before deciding how wicked you are I'd very much like to know the answer to that one. And of course I would like to know why you should want to protect your husband's family if they are making such difficulties for you."

At these words she drew further back, her smile fading, her expression becoming serious. He watched her over the top of his glass as he sipped again.

"I think they came to rob me," she said.

"Of what?"

"The paper – the valuation, perhaps."

"Won't they get a copy?"

"There is much trouble and some things are not certain," she said. "Also – they come to frighten me." When Mannering did not speak she went on: "They have attempted this before. They think if I am frightened I will do what they want."

"And what do they want?"

"Two thirds of the value of the Collection."

"And have they frightened you?" asked Mannering.

"But of course. Many times. That is why I want to sell the

Collection quickly and take the money with me to another country, where I shall be safe from them."

"But you've never been frightened enough to give them what they want?"

"Of course not!" There was anger in her voice. "Would you expect that of me?"

"I don't know you well enough yet to say," he replied. "I don't even know if you are a wicked woman, remember!" His eyes laughed and laughter sprang back to hers. "And I don't know why, under such circumstances, you should try to protect his family."

He wondered what she would answer, whether he should have waited for a while and not risked spoiling the happy mood. Certainly the laughter died, and she frowned – as he had once seen her frown behind dark glasses.

Then, she said: "For my husband's sake, Mr. Mannering. For his memory. He was a good man. He loved his two sons. Is that something you can understand, or does it seem to you a pretence, a lie?"

9

Dinner for Two

Mannering finished his drink, and moving forward placed a hand lightly beneath her chin, tilting her head back slightly so that he could see the fullness of her beauty. She did not attempt to shift her position or to look away from him; there was defiance in her eyes but he did not think there was falsehood.

"It is something I would like very much to believe," he said.

"Is it so hard to believe the truth?"

"Is it so easy to be sure what the truth is?" he countered. "Lucille, I tell you I want very much to believe it. Perhaps I shall find that possible when I know the whole story."

She drew in a deep breath, nodded, moved away and echoed: "Perhaps, yes. And perhaps it will be easier when you are not hungry! Tell me, please, are you a domesticated man?"

He followed her change of mood unhesitatingly.

"Well, if you mean can I find my way about a kitchen – yes."

"Bravo! I will be grateful for a little help, a very little help, with plates and knives and forks. In ten minutes, in *five* minutes you will be eating!" She took his hand and led him across the hall to a smaller dining-room full of books and *objets d'art*. From this she led him to a kitchen which would have made Lorna green with envy.

"From the refrigerator, please, the white wine. Also the butter."

She opened the door of an eye-level oven and pulled a shelf forward, then drew out a dark green dish – his first indication that they were to have roast duck à l'orange.

"Now please," she said, "in the larder there is some bread, please cut what you think we shall need and place it in the basket."

The bread was a golden brown French loaf, and the knife lay on the board.

"Now from the refrigerator some melon," she went on, shutting the door of the oven, and moving towards him with two dishes she seemed to have taken from nowhere. As he did as she directed, she declared gaily: "Now no more kitchen work for you – we start!"

The food was more than excellent, it was superb. Lucille ate with the single-minded attention of the gourmet, and they said very little. He gave her more of the duck, and took some himself. She preferred the white wine, a Moutrachet, he the red, from a château he knew only vaguely; but the flavour was perfect. An iced pudding followed.

At last they were done, and she said: "You would like coffee and some brandy, I am sure. You go please and prepare the brandy, I will bring the coffee."

"Do let me help—"

"There is no need," she said. "Please."

He went back to the first room he had entered and found glasses, Martell, Napoleon and Courvoisier brandy, on a glass-covered table. Soon she came in with the coffee, which she placed on a small table between two comfortable armchairs.

"So," she said. "You enjoy?"

"It was a perfect meal."

"In spite of everything else?"

"All I was interested in was you – and the food," Mannering added, laughing.

"You are ver' gallant, M'sieu Mannering."

"Lucille," he said, picking up her glass and handing it to her, "either we are going to become good friends or not friends at all, so – should we be formal?"

"Formal?" she echoed, looking puzzled, until suddenly her face cleared and she laughed. "No, John! No, we do not have to be formal." Her eyes seemed to take on the colour of the brandy as she raised her glass. A moment later she poured coffee, then pulled a cushion close and sat on it so that she could look up slightly at Mannering. She looked at him for a long time and he did not even try to guess what was passing through her mind.

One thing he knew: it had been a long time since he had felt so absolutely contented.

It could only have been minutes but it seemed an age when she said quietly: "Now, John, the time has come to talk. Has it not?"

He wanted to say "No." He longed just to sit here and watch her, feeling the warmth from the brandy steal through his veins, knowing that soon – or at least some time not very far distant – they would draw closer together. It was the only, it was the natural, it was the inevitable sequel to what had happened and was still happening.

He almost said: I don't want to talk about anything, Lucille.

He did say: "Yes, I'm afraid it has."

"And I have to convince you that I tell the truth," she said, "and first, you wish to know why I watched you in the way I did."

He had forgotten that question.

"Yes," he said.

"It is very simple. I knew you were the one who was to value the Collection. I knew that my step-sons wanted the Collection. I wished to make sure you did not visit them, or they visit you. In the beginning I expected them to, but they did not. Perhaps it was because Mr. Harcourt had convinced them that you were incorruptible, but for me – I must satisfy this for myself."

"You could have used a private inquiry agency."

"Oh, but I did so," she answered.

"To watch *me*?" Was it possible others had been trailing him and he had not been aware of it? Surely Bristow—

Her eyes were brimming over with laughter as if she understood what was passing through his mind, and she waited long enough to get the full savour from that situation before saying: "But no, John. To watch my step-sons!"

He found himself laughing, and then was surprised because she began to draw her brows together, apparently not thinking it funny. She sat with the brandy glass cupped in her hands for a few moments, and then remarked pensively: "They did not come to see you. You did not meet. I wonder how you would get on if you did meet?"

Mannering said: "Why did you expect them to come to see me?"

"Oh, I expected them to try to bribe you to put a very low valuation on the Collection so that you could advise me to sell at a very low price. Oh, they are scoundrels," she went on, smiling now. "So was their father, but he was a darling scoundrel, whereas his sons – I hope you will not like them," she finished abruptly.

"I may never meet them," Mannering said.

"I think you will," declared Lucille. "Do not ask me why, but I think you will meet them. Now, John, what more is there to tell you? That they have accused me of murdering my sweetheart Ezra – oh, it is ridiculous, but they have. He died of a heart attack, what you call a cerebral haemorrhage also, and it was very sudden. How they think I could cause such a thing I do not know, but they are funny people." She shrugged her shoulders as if accepting such 'funniness' as part of her life. "Also, they accuse me of having lovers by the dozen! In that there is a little, just a little, more truth." She put her head on one side. "Does that not shock you?"

"Should I be shocked?"

"You have the reputation of being a one-woman man," declared Lucille, and mischief glinted in her eyes. "So perhaps you are shocked. Not with other people, no?" She frowned. "I mean you are not shocked if other people take lovers but—" She broke off and stood up. She had been sitting in what must have been an awkward position for rising but she was on her feet in a single, effortless movement, and began to walk about the room;

now there was a touch of the feline in her; of the leopard, of the wild cat, her hair and her eyes flashing a tawny gold. "I promised to tell the truth, I tell the truth, not because it is a matter to discuss but because in one way it explains the attitude of the brothers. You will listen?"

"Of course."

"Good! Then it is so, I have taken lovers. I am not yet old but Ezra was old and he was not a lover, he was what do you say—?"

"Impotent?"

"So. It was not his fault, he was a sick man, soon after we were married he began to have the heart attacks. That is one reason why the family blame me – they say *I* gave him these attacks. If I did, I do not know how. It was a very good relationship between Ezra and me. He was not a jealous man, he knew that sometimes I needed more than he could give me. He asked me only one thing: an impossible thing, but only one." She came to rest in front of him and sank down on the cushion so that she knelt in front of him, only a foot or two away. She rested her ringless hands on her knees as she went on as if driven by a compulsion she could not deny. "He asked me not to fall in love." She closed her eyes and began to sway a little on her knees as she repeated: "How is it possible for a man or a woman to command themselves *not* to fall in love? I could promise him I would not, but how could I be sure? I could promise him I would never leave him, and this promise I could keep but—"

She broke off, stopped swaying, and opened her eyes. Her head was tilted back as if in invitation for his lips; and hers were parted very slightly so that he could just see her teeth.

Mannering said huskily: "So you fell in love."

Slowly, very slowly, she shook her head, saying in a voice which seemed to come from far away: "No, I did not fall in love while Ezra was alive, but if I had met the man earlier then I would have done. It was his death which introduced us." She smiled, and paused, then standing up with another effortless movement, began to walk around the room talking in a much more light-hearted way.

"No, John, you know everything except one thing, which is important – and perhaps you can judge for yourself. I am supposed to be mad. *Une imbécile.*" She stood in front of him making the face children make when they pretend to be a bogey man. "You understand? I am not right in the head. This is what my stepsons are saying, so that they can discredit me. Everything, everything they can do to make me give them the Collection they will do. *Do you understand?*" Now she stood with her hands raised in front of her, the lists clenched. "You count, please. I am the murderess. I am the seductress. I am the imbecile. I should be shut away in some prison or perhaps in some home. And I do not know whether they could succeed in this or not, so I want to sell the Collection for as much money as I can get quickly and leave England. *Soon.* That is why I want you to help me, that is why I have asked you here and given you the dinner I cooked for you with such thought, and told you all the truth."

She dropped into her chair now, and covered her face with her hands. She was a-tremble from head to foot and it was all he could do to prevent himself from going to her, picking her up, holding and comforting her.

Why didn't he?

Bristow's face seemed to hover in front of his mind and Bristow's voice to echo in his ears. "Why don't you, John?"

Why didn't he?

He sat without moving, looking at her; shaken emotionally, but still not entirely bereft of the power of reasoning. She could be acting. Or she could simply be being herself.

"Lucille," he said, "your step-sons will do all this and you still don't want them to be proved scoundrels?"

"I do not," she said huskily.

"It makes no sense."

"Am I the one who must always make sense?" she demanded, her face still covered by her hands.

"Why did you buy the emerald tiara this morning?"

She started violently, snatched her hands from her face and stared at him in astonishment; he had no doubt at all that she had been taken completely by surprise. She actually tried to speak but could not find words until he insisted: "Could you afford it? And whether you could or not why did you buy it?"

She said simply: "It was beautiful."

"Did you buy it because it was beautiful?"

She did not answer at first, but looked at him with a kind of defiance which grew bolder as the seconds passed. By her manner he knew that something would come like a bolt from the blue, and he had a feeling that it would be the truth: that all along she had told the truth, but not all of it.

At last, she said: "If I tell you, you may not like the reason."

"On the other hand, I may."

"So," she said, in that attractive way of hers. "I saw you come along Hart Row and I saw you look at the emeralds and I saw your face and I knew the truth: you had a great passion for them, great love, great desire. So, I bought the jewels because I thought some of those things you felt for them you might also feel for me. I did not wish to tell you this but I must do so now, John. I have fallen in love with you. Almost from the first moment I saw you, it happened. I cannot explain. I ask you for nothing, but I tell you truly, John. I love you."

10

Woman in Love

There was a deep silence, broken at last by Lucille who said in a strained voice: "Why do you not say something? Is it such an insult that I should fall in love with you? Are you going to make me wish I had not told you?"

Mannering leaned forward and stretched out his hands; she took them, hesitantly, searching his face for some clue to his thoughts. He was seeking desperately for the right thing to say; trying as desperately to still the thunder in his own breast. Beyond her was an image of his wife as she had stood on that morning when he had hurried back for the report on the Peek Collection and she had been waiting at the door of the lift.

"Lucille," he said, his voice not quite steady, "I've never promised my wife that I won't ever fall in love with another woman. But it might—might break her heart if I did, and I don't think I could do anything which I knew could hurt her."

Fiercely, Lucille demanded: "But if you had no wife?"

"I would have found out who you were a long time ago," Mannering said.

"Why didn't you?"

"I dared not."

"Dared not," Lucille breathed. "Because—" She broke off and for a moment her grip on his hands tightened. "There is no need to explain more. I understand. I understand even if I do not have to think you are right."

Mannering didn't speak.

"John," Lucille said, "because of what I have told you – because of the feeling between us – will it be impossible to help me?"

"I must help you," Mannering said.

"And you *will*?"

"Even if all the police say you are a murderess and all the psychiatrists say you are not right in the head and even if I knew you had a thousand lovers, I will help you."

"You will buy the Collection?" she cried.

"It wouldn't be helping you if I bought the Collection, or found a buyer," he said. "I want to know the real reason why you are being persecuted. Why your husband's sons are behaving like this. Why a man should telephone me this evening and warn me that you destroy your lovers and kill your husbands!" He took her hands again as anger flared up in her eyes. "Where do they live, these step-sons of yours?"

"That is a word I hate!"

"Where do they live?"

"One of them lives in the house at Ealing where Ezra and I used to live, and the other lives close by here, in Hampstead. I will give you their addresses, but John – what will you do?"

"I don't know yet," Mannering said. "Will you write the addresses down?" As she moved to a small secretaire, he went on: "Do Harcourt, Pace and Pace represent them, as well?"

"Not now," she said.

"When did they stop?"

"When it became obvious six months ago that we could not settle anything amicably, they went to another firm. I do not know who they are, but perhaps I could find out."

"I'll find out," Mannering said, taking the slip of paper from her. He stood up, and looked down at her, adding: "One more thing, Lucille."

"What is that?" she asked.

"No more following me."

"I will promise that, if you will promise to see me sometimes."

"On business, I shall have to!" He felt his heart lift as her eyes danced. "And still another thing: if you have any threats, any trouble, any visits from your step-sons let me know at once."

"That I will gladly do," she said. "You cannot imagine how it will feel not to be alone again."

"You won't be alone," he said gruffly.

He moved almost without realising what he was doing, took her in his arms, crushed her to him, crushed her lips – and then suddenly released her and swung away, out of the room, out of the flat and down the stairs.

She did not follow.

When he reached the street he looked up at her window and saw her there, but she did not wave or move.

He went to his car, started the engine and eased out of the parking place, came within an ace of scraping the bumper of another car, and turned out of Northcote Square without looking – until an oncoming car's headlights flashed and horn blared, and he jammed on his brakes. "Not fit to drive," he jeered at himself, and edged round the corner towards St. John's Wood Road and found an easy parking place.

He pulled into it and took out a cigarette, realised he had his headlights full on, and turned them off savagely. "How the devil can I be sure she's not lying?" he asked the empty car, and then a moment later said harshly: "I know she's not lying." He half-finished the cigarette and then stubbed it out. Feeling calmer, he started off again, but as he did so a police car turned the corner and he flashed his light at it. The car pulled across to him, and the young man he had seen twice before got out, exclaiming: "Mr. Mannering! We were just coming to see if you were still at Mrs. Peek's."

"Why?" asked Mannering, much more mildly than he felt.

"We wondered if you would, come and have a look at those two johnnies we brought away," said the police constable. "Just to see if you've ever seen them before. Would you care to follow us?"

"Certainly. To Divisional H.Q.?"

"Yes. It's only a short distance, sir."

He had wanted to know what story the two men had told, and needed some distraction to force him to think of other things than Lucille. At least his control of the car was all right now, and he followed the police car without difficulty until they pulled up outside the Divisional Headquarters. Two uniformed men were on duty outside, three long-haired youths were in the charge room. The bright young policeman led Mannering upstairs, turned left along a narrow passage and then tapped at a door marked: *Superintendent*. A voice called "Come in" and Mannering was ushered in to see a youthful-looking man at the big, flat-topped desk and Bill Bristow, standing beside him.

"Mr. Mannering," the Superintendent said. "I'm Hardy, James Hardy." They shook hands. "We couldn't be more glad about the two men you caught for us tonight. Both men have records as long as your arm. Even Bill Bristow remembers them, they go as far back as that."

Everyone laughed, dutifully.

"And John," Bristow said, "they've admitted being paid to attack you."

"Did they know why?" asked Mannering.

"If they know why they haven't said so." Hardy, who looked a very tough, rock-hard individual with bright blue eyes, had a crisp, authoritative voice. "They say they were given five hundred pounds apiece."

"So the price on my head is a thousand pounds," said Mannering, with an attempt at lightness. "Dead or alive?"

"I think, dead," put in Bristow.

"And *I* don't think anyone would pay a thousand pounds simply to have you knocked on the head," agreed Hardy. When he smiled it was with a kind of false, wolfish brilliance. "Why should anyone want to kill you so much, Mr. Mannering?"

"I only wish I knew," Mannering said. "Bill – what brought you here?"

"Quite a coincidence," Hardy answered for Bristow. "I was a Chief Inspector at Ealing when Ezra Peek died, and I actually handled the inquiries into his death. I knew him and his family well. So when Bill went over to Ealing to check, they referred him to me. It was a case of the long arm of the law of coincidence working together."

"Was there any suspicion of foul play over Peek's death?" asked Mannering.

"There was talk," answered Hardy. "Anonymous telephone calls, accusations against his wife, enough to make a thorough investigation necessary. The conclusion was that Ezra Peek had died of natural causes. There were some suggestions that he had brought this on himself prematurely by marrying a comparatively young woman. There were others that his wife encouraged him to excessive activity—"

Mannering asked flatly: "Sexual?"

"Never more than by implication. No. Gardening, golf, walking, that kind of thing. But he had always gardened and golfed and was a mountain climber and potholer in his youth. So the rumours added up to gossip – no more."

Mannering felt a surge of relief spreading through him, until Hardy went on quietly: "There was one possibility which we considered, which wasn't proved and I doubt if it could ever be proved now. That his medication was either held back or diluted. He was on a fairly regular dosage of digitalis. He either dosed himself or was dosed by his wife. But we found no evidence that less than the usual supplies had been bought, we found no surplus at the house. There was nothing at all for us to act on. The coroner's verdict was natural causes. And until tonight I hadn't given it any more thought."

"Was the rest of Peek's family really hostile to his wife?"

"Hostile is a mild word. They hated her."

"Did you discover any reasons? Material reasons?"

"Only that she would get some of the money they thought should be theirs," answered Hardy. "I can't pretend that the step-sons were a nice couple. Took after the first wife more than the old man, I'm told." Hardy leaned back in his chair and eyed Mannering thoughtfully. "Are you working for Mrs. Peek?"

"Yes."

Bristow looked more relaxed than he had since Mannering had come into the office, while Hardy asked: "Why? Are you selling the Collection?"

"I'm trying to find out why the step-sons are so anxious to get it," Mannering said.

"You wouldn't be tempted to poach on our preserves, would you?" asked Hardy, with a steely tone in his voice.

"I wouldn't hesitate to do so for a moment, if I thought it necessary," Mannering answered, with a disarming smile. "Mrs. Peek is so scared of her husband's family that she's prepared to sell the Collection for a tenth of its value, in order to get away from them. I doubt if it's a police matter yet, but—"

"Do you think the attempt to kill you was to stop you from helping her?"

"It could have been."

"Then it's a police matter all right," Hardy said grimly. He stood up, glanced at Bristow and then went on to Mannering in a different tone of voice, one touched almost with apology. "There—ah—is one thing you should perhaps know about Lucille Peek if you are trying to help her."

"What is that?" asked Mannering.

"She takes a very liberal attitude on sex."

"Yes," Mannering said, more lightly than he felt. "So she told me. Apparently it quite shocked her husband's family!" He allowed the others time to recover from this broadside before going on: "Will the two assailants be charged in the morning?"

"Yes – you'll be in court, won't you?"

"Yes," replied Mannering in turn, and then he asked easily: "Do you know the Peek solicitors – Harcourt, Pace and Pace?"

"Yes," answered Hardy briskly.

"Do you know *he* suffers from heart trouble and nearly collapsed this afternoon? I wonder if he has regular digitalis treatment, and whether anybody tampers with his doses."

"I can tell you that he has the same ailment and the same form of treatment as Ezra Peek had," Bristow said. "I managed to have a word with one of his managing clerks. He had these short-term collapses quite often."

"Surely that *must* be coincidence," Hardy exclaimed.

"Well, it certainly might be," Mannering said.

A few minutes later he was outside the police station with Bristow, whose car was parked behind the building, while Mannering's was at the kerb. Neither man felt like talking, but Mannering said lightly: "She's quite a woman, isn't she, Bill?"

"I have a feeling you ought to be very careful with her," declared Bristow cautiously. He laughed, in the way people do when they wish to ameliorate the seriousness of what they had said.

Mannering took the wheel of his Allard and drove towards the West End, the quickest way to reach his Chelsea home. It was now half-past ten and Lorna would be home. He was back at the question: how much to tell her? All? Or nothing? Before deciding, he wanted more time to consider his own reactions, to be quite sure how he felt. And the very fact that he took it seriously enough to need to think seriously appalled him.

It would be pointless to put off going home.

He smiled grimly to himself as he parked the car and went back along Green Street towards his house. Lorna *was* at home, there were lights shining from the top windows. He took out his keys to open the front door, and was suddenly aware of how similar this situation was to the one at Northcote Square. The feeling came so strongly that he actually turned round.

A man was leaping towards him: and in his hand was a knife.

A split second later, and it would have been too late: the blade would have buried itself in his back. As it was, he shot out his left leg and caught the wrist of the hand in which the knife was held. He heard a gasp, saw the man stagger away, then was aware of a second man leaping towards him from the cover of parked cars. He flung himself forward, suddenly certain that this man too, held a knife.

On that instant a car swung into the street from King's Road, headlights carving a wide beam. The man with whom he was struggling pulled himself free, and both assailants raced towards the other end of the street. The police siren blared out as the car passed Mannering, who stood in the entrance to the house, breathing hard, aware of something warm on the back of his hand and on his forehead. He looked down. The street lighting was good enough to show blood welling up out of a cut; there must be a cut on his forehead, too. He fumbled for a handkerchief. The police siren faded but the car had not stopped: he wondered if the men had escaped.

He opened the street door and passed through the lobby, to the lift. Catching a glimpse of himself in a wall mirror he was appalled, for one side of his forehead and much of his cheek was glistening with blood. If Lorna saw him like this, without warning, she would have a shock which might upset her for days. Yet she may have heard the lift; all he could do was dab at his cheek and temple with a padded handkerchief as he opened the door of the flat.

The hall light and the kitchen light were on; but there was no sound. Had she dropped off to sleep while waiting? He went quietly to the kitchen and saw a note propped up against a teapot on a tray which was always ready. It read:

Darling, I've come home with such a sickening headache I'm going straight to bed. Forgive.

His first reaction was that he would not have to tell her a thing tonight, would have a chance first to think and then decide on what to say.

11

Relief . . .

Mannering felt an intense relief.

It was absurd, the whole affair was ridiculous, but the relief was real enough to make him forget everything else for a few minutes. He went into the bathroom, turned on the taps, and gazed at himself in the mirror – lord, he was in a mess! Blood had run down to his shirt collar, but the damage was not as much as it looked. He stripped to the waist then bathed the cuts in his forehead and the back of his hand. When cleaned they looked little more than scratches, but if he had caught the full force of either blow – phew!

Looking for a roll of bandage the thought flashed across his mind that the police car must have been following him, that other police might be here at any moment. He spun round, hearing the faint whine of the lift. As he moved into the hall the doors opened and two police patrolmen stepped out. Mannering put a finger to his lips and as they drew nearer, said softly: "I don't want to wake my wife."

"Quite understand, sir," the first man said. He looked little more than a boy but the other must be in his thirties.

"You'll need some help with that cut," he said authoritatively.

"Oh, it's nothing," Mannering said.

"I'd like to have a look at it, sir." They went together to the bathroom, all three large men making hardly a sound. The older of the others washed his hands beneath the tap and then examined Mannering's temple and forehead. "They really were after you, sir, weren't they? Second time tonight, I understand."

"So it's been broadcast." Mannering watched the smaller man open the bathroom cabinet.

"Only to the police, sir. We were on the lookout for your car, just came to see you were all safely tucked up in bed."

"Did you get them?"

"They had a car waiting at the end of the street, with a driver," declared the other. "This will sting a bit, sir."

"Sting on. So they both got away."

"We've another car after them and there's a general call. With a bit of luck we'll pick them up before long." As he busied himself with the cuts, there was a brisk efficiency in all he did, and Mannering gave him top marks for first-aid. "Did you recognise them, sir?"

"I didn't get a real look at them, but – no, I don't think we were old friends."

The younger man chuckled. "You can say that again."

"Care to make a statement?" asked the older man. He fastened a bandage in position carefully and then turned to Mannering's hand.

"I was about to enter the house when two men attacked me."

"Any idea why, sir?"

"None at all – unless it is connected with the earlier attack, and it's hardly likely two lots would be after me in one night."

"You can't tell, with a gentleman of your reputation. Any ideas why the other attack was made?"

"None. And I've made a statement about that to St. John's Wood Superintendent," Mannering said. He watched the other fasten another bandage over his hand, and said warmly: "I don't know what I would have done without your help."

"Feel O.K., sir?"

"Tired, that's all."

"Can we get you anything? Cup of tea, or—"

"Do you know, tea would be just right," Mannering said. "And

I'm going to use the spare room tonight – my wife went to bed early with a headache."

The policeman asked: "Have you seen her since you came back, sir?"

"No, but—"

Mannering stopped, and the possible significance of the question hit him like a sledge-hammer. For a moment dizziness swept over him, then, shaking it off, he moved swiftly towards the larger bedroom. The door was ajar but there was no light on. He pushed the door wider, and peered at the bed, and now there was sufficient light to show Lorna lying on her side, her face serene and peaceful. He backed out, saying: "You had me scared for a moment!"

"Just as well to be sure, sir," said the older man comfortably.

The other was already making tea . . .

Ten minutes afterwards they left him in the spare room, already in pyjamas, a bottle of aspirins on the tea-tray as well as tea and biscuits. "Are you domesticated?" Lucille had asked him, and he found himself smiling. These two policemen certainly were. And the older man really knew his business. Mannering drank a cup of tea, started on another, then pushed the tray away, suddenly caught in a yawn which seemed to lift the top of his head right off and to start it aching furiously. Yet he could not have been awake and aware of that for more than five minutes before he dropped off.

"Bill," said Superintendent Hardy to Bristow on the telephone, "two more men were waiting outside Mannering's place to attack him when he got home."

Bristow, who had just got home, demanded: "Was he hurt?"

"Not seriously."

"Get the men?"

"Not when I last heard," answered Hardy. "Have you any idea what all this attempted violence is about?"

"I don't know a thing more than either Mannering or I told you," Bristow assured him. "But my God, I'm going to find out!

Four attackers in one night! Are you having the Chelsea house watched?"

"I'm not, but the Division over there is, and the Yard's taken over," Hardy told him. "My only concern now is Lucille Peek, and I'll have her watched and followed wherever she goes. If you get the slightest inkling of what it's all about you'll let me or someone at the Yard know, won't you?"

"Yes," Bristow said. "I certainly will."

He replaced the receiver and stood for a few moments in the hallway of his flat on Putney Hill, where he and his wife had lived for over twenty years. The call had come through only a few minutes after he had got in. His wife was reading in bed, and when he joined her she simply glanced up and smiled vaguely before going back to the pages.

He faced what seemed to be a simple fact: the moment Mannering had discovered the identity of the woman in dark glasses, these vicious attacks had begun. There was another, equally unarguable fact: they had started within a few hours of his giving Norman Harcourt and the woman the final valuation figures for the Peek Collection.

All his years of training and experience of Scotland Yard seemed to scream at Bristow with one question: *why?*

He found himself asking what he knew Hardy and everyone on the Metropolitan Police Force was asking: Did John Mannering know more than he had yet admitted? Getting ready for bed Bristow ran through everything he could remember, and everything brought the same answer: in this, Mannering had levelled with him completely; he was as baffled as Bristow.

What other 'coincidences' had there been? Repeat: the violence had started after Mannering had identified Lucille; it had started after Mannering had taken the valuation. Was there anything else—God! The sudden seizure of Norman Harcourt only an hour after he had realised the enormous value of the Collection and at the very moment when he had been about to tell Mannering!

Could he have been silenced?

The withdrawal of certain drugs could cause a seizure; or the administration of other drugs. Way back in his mind there was a recollection of a drug which could induce—

An overdose of digitalis would bring on an attack in some patients.

Bristow turned and looked at his bedside clock as his wife shut her book, and with a placid "Goodnight, dear", settled down. It was five minutes to one. Much too late to start making inquiries, but first thing in the morning he would start checking. First, how Norman Harcourt was: second, what drug *could* have brought on that attack at the crucial moment.

Bristow turned over, willing himself to sleep; but he was awake for a long time.

Norman Harcourt was not sleeping, either.

He lay between life and death, with nurses round his bed and a doctor in constant attendance. He was a widower, no relatives were by his side, but one of his younger partners was, as anxious as if he were a son.

Lucille Peek slept, unaware of police watching both the back and front of her house. She looked quite lovely. On the bedside table was a newspaper-cutting with a photograph of Mannering, and, close to it, several smaller photographs cut out of the glossy magazines which served the arts and the antique businesses; it was surprising how many articles she had been able to find about him.

There was also a photograph of his wife, a beautiful woman as different from Lucille as two women could be.

On the dressing-table stood a wig which she used occasionally for evenings, so skilfully made that it always appeared to be her own hair, dressed in a different style. It faced her. There was a faint light from the passage which she left on all night and this showed not only the wig on the head-stand, but also its reflection in the dressing-table mirror.

On the wig, was the emerald tiara.

Even in this faint light the green jewels glowed, a lambent light which was like the light reflected from the eyes of a hundred cats; green, glowing eyes which were still for one minute and then seemed to move but did not really move at all. When she woke in the morning this would be the first thing she would see; and, on the same instant, she would see a portrait of John Mannering, taken from a magazine which, only two years before, had published an article on Quinn's; which inevitably meant an article, also, on Mannering.

Mannering woke to the sound of a closing door, lay for a few moments not sure where he was but aware that the room was unfamiliar. Outside, a murky daylight showed against the windows; it was November, and to be daylight it must be getting late. Nine? He turned to look at his bedside clock; it was half-past ten. What on earth had he been doing to sleep at this hour?

Suddenly he thought: Am I at Lucille's?

The thought was hardly in his mind when he realised he was in the spare room of his own flat, and memory flooded back. He felt tenderness at his temple and the back of his left hand: nothing worse.

Lorna must have come in, seen him, seen the patches, left him to rest. He pushed the bedclothes back and got out of bed cautiously, relieved to find he was all in one piece. His head ached a little but nothing like it had done the night before. He called: "Anyone at home?"

Immediately there were footsteps and Lorna appeared at the end of the passage, wearing a smock which meant she had been painting in the studio.

"John," she said severely, "back to bed while I make some tea."

He drew her to him and kissed her cheek, a chaste good-morning kiss like a thousand others. He saw the anxiety in her eyes but let her go and hurry back into the kitchen while he plunged his face in cold water in the bathroom which led off the spare room. He tapped both bandages gingerly, and the cuts were no more than tender, and if there were any inflammation they would be sore. Bless that policeman! He was actually back in bed, hitching the pillows up behind him, when Lorna came in with the same tea-tray the police had used not so many hours before. She put this on a nearby table, and sat at the foot of the bed.

"You *look* all right," she admitted.

"No bloodshot eyes? No signs of dissolution? No—"

"Darling," she said, "it isn't funny."

"How much do you know?"

"Everything that matters I should think," she said. "You were attacked when you went to Mrs. Peek's flat last night, and again when you came here." As she said: "Mrs. Peek's flat," she began to pour out his tea, as if she did not want to see his expression: or else did not want him to see hers.

She knew where he had been for dinner. She—

He hadn't had any opportunity to tell her, anyhow. His heart stopped hammering, and he realised that the decision to tell, or not to tell, her had been made for him – by Bristow.

She handed him a cup of steaming hot tea. He sipped in silence for a few seconds, and then asked: "Did Bill tell you how much her Collection is worth?"

"Nearly three and a half million pounds," she answered. "I could understand—" She broke off and laughed. "What on earth am I doing, trying to think for you when you're only half-awake!"

"Your thoughts are often clearer than mine," he said. "Think on. Aloud!"

She leaned forward, rearranging the cups on the tray. Was it his imagination or was there something different in her manner? A preoccupation with thoughts she had no intention of 'thinking aloud'?

"I could understand it if they'd tried to prevent you from valuing the Collection if they – someone – wanted it to be under-valued, but why now, darling? What motive could anyone possibly have? Unless—"

Again she broke off and this time there was no doubt at all in his mind that she was holding something back. He wondered whether he should try to make her talk or whether he should just leave whatever it was alone. Quite suddenly he knew that he wanted to know, that it was not good to hold secrets so that the other might wonder and even worry or fret.

So he said quietly: "Unless what, darling?"

"Unless someone is jealous of you," she said. "Unless someone thinks you can influence her and influence what she does with the Collection. Is that possible?"

12

Jealousy?

Mannering stopped hearing what his wife said after the first sentence. "Unless someone is jealous of you." Who could have put that thought in Lorna's mind? Jealous? He knew that he looked as startled, and as shocked, as he felt. Lorna shot him a look, limpid, and much too innocent.

"Could you influence her, darling?"

Mannering drew a deep breath.

"It hadn't occurred to me," he said. "Why on earth should you think—?" He broke off, not wanting to complete the sentence with the obvious ". . . anyone would be jealous of me?" He finished his tea, which was still hot: that showed how little time had passed since they had started talking.

"Another?" Lorna asked.

"I think I need a strong whisky and soda!"

"I'll cook you some bacon and eggs and make some coffee," she said; there was no question, she was laughing at him; well, half-laughing. "Darling," she went on, "I think Mrs. Peek – Lucille – in the way rich and capricious women can be, is infatuated with you. Isn't she?"

"Could be," Mannering said uncomfortably.

"Ah, my feminine intuition wins again," Lorna said with a note of triumph. "After all, it didn't need much of it. She *has* followed you about quite a lot, you know. I haven't been on the lookout for her but even I've seen her at least a dozen times."

"Dark glasses and all."

"What's she like without them?"

"A lot of people would say she was beautiful."

"What do *you* say?"

"She's beautiful all right," Mannering said stiffly. "Lorna—"

Lorna said: "She is your client, isn't she?"

"Yes."

"And not only because she's infatuated with you?"

"In spite of that," answered Mannering.

"So you'll have to do whatever you can to help her," Lorna said, "and if she were an old woman of eighty or a teenager, or a man or a boy you wouldn't feel you had to go into explanations about your relationship with them, would you?"

"No," Mannering admitted.

"You'd ask me to help if I could, but unless you thought I could you probably wouldn't talk much about the case, would you?"

"No."

"Very well, then"—Lorna took his cup and kissed him lightly on the forehead—"just promise me one thing." She paused and he knew she was deliberately tantalising him, yet he could not imagine what she was going to ask, and he thought, in a flash mental vision, of what Lucille had said about some promises which could not be kept, some requests—demands?—which were beyond the human being to command. He waited, heart thumping, as the laughter faded from Lorna's eyes, and she went on: "Promise to let me know if I can help. About the Collection, about the case, about Lucille – anything."

With an enormous sense of release Mannering replied: "Yes, my darling, I will."

"And don't get yourself killed," added Lorna.

That was the first time emotion broke through, reflected in the slight huskiness of her voice, and the sudden dread which showed in her eyes. Then she stood up, lifted the tray, and turned towards the door.

"Breakfast in half-an-hour. Does that sound good?"

It sounded good all right. It was good.

He blessed the tact with which Lorna, leaving the coffee to percolate, went up to the studio; he would call up to her before he left. He ate with relish, marvelling at his wife, wondering how she really felt, what she guessed, whether she thought that he and Lucille were lovers. It was nearly half-past eleven when he finished, and he was in the hall when the telephone bell rang again. He picked up an extension.

"Mannering."

Bristow said: "Norman Harcourt's dying. He's asking for you. How soon can you be ready?"

"I am ready. Where does he live?"

"In Wimbledon – Number 15, Common Way," answered Bristow. "I'll arrange for a police car to lead you if you'll be at the top of Putney Hill in fifteen minutes."

"I'll be there," Mannering said, moving towards the lift entrance the moment the receiver was down. "Darling, I'm off." He heard her footsteps and she appeared at the hatch, kneeling down to look at him.

"Old Harcourt's in a bad way," he said, "and asking for me."

"Call me whenever you can. I'll be in all day."

"I will."

He blew her a kiss and then hurried out of the flat, recognising plainclothes men on duty as he reached his car, remembering the times when they would have been waiting there not to watch over his safety but to trap him as a suspected criminal. An age away. Turning into King's Road he saw a police car heading towards him from Chelsea High Street, and it followed close behind. The authorities were evidently taking the previous attacks on him seriously. He had a good run at traffic lights except at the top of Putney High Street, where a funeral cortege delayed him. At the top of the hill, another police car stood waiting, and pulled out as Mannering approached.

Soon they turned off the main road, and the police car ahead made several sharp swings before entering a wide street with a sign reading clearly: Common Way. This was part of the Victorian era, only one small block of modern flats having so far encroached on the big, red brick houses which had once been the norm. Most of the entrances were wide and well-kept, most had big gates; trees here were tall and stately, the shrubs thick with rhododendron, bay and laurel.

The police driver waved, and slowed down as he pointed to an open gateway; on the gate-post the number FIFTEEN was clearly marked. Mannering turned into this. Three other cars were in a spacious driveway which encircled a patch of shrubs. The house was taller than most and had a round turret room with a spire. As Mannering approached the wide porch, the door opened and a youthful-looking man asked: "Mr. Mannering?"

"Yes."

"I am Charles Pace, one of Mr. Harcourt's partners." He turned and led the way towards a passage at the side of the stairs, talking as he went. "It is very good of you to come, although whether Mr. Harcourt will recognise you or become coherent I would not like to say." He stopped at a fairly recently installed lift, adding: "This saved him from walking up the stairs, which latterly became such a problem for him." He stood aside for Mannering to enter, followed, and pressed a button marked 2; there were four buttons in all. The lift went up very slowly. Mannering began to wonder if they would ever get there.

At last it stopped – opposite the door of what proved to be a large bedroom at the front of the house, with huge bay windows at which the curtains were half-drawn. Huge pieces of mahogany furniture stood against the walls, one of which was a four-poster bed on which Norman Harcourt lay, breathing heavily.

On one side was an elderly man; on the other, a much younger one.

"Dr. Medway and Dr. Gill," said Pace in a quiet but perfectly audible voice. "Mr. Mannering, gentlemen."

The others nodded. Harcourt gave no sign at all that he had heard the name or indeed heard anything. A young Jamaican nurse came out of a bathroom which led off the room, but did not approach. Mannering felt as if he were in the presence of death and was appalled by the change in the sick man's appearance. Yesterday he had been fresh-faced, wholesome-looking, a dignified seventy. Now his face was grey and drawn, his eyes sunken.

"Norman," said the older doctor, Medway, in a clear voice, "Mr. Mannering has come to see you."

How could that corpse-like figure possibly hear? Certainly Harcourt did not stir, but Medway was not put off and, leaning a little closer, he repeated: "Norman, Mr. Mannering has come to see you."

Harcourt *did* react.

His eyes flickered open. He turned his face towards the sound of the voice, and his lips moved.

"Mannering. Must—talk—Mannering," he muttered.

Medway touched Mannering's arm and he leaned closer to the sick man's face, speaking in a clear, normal voice.

"I am here, Mr. Harcourt. This *is* Mannering. How can I help you?"

The ashen lips moved again.

"Must speak—Mannering."

"I *am* Mannering," Mannering said. He took the old man's hand in his own and went on: "We met in your office, yesterday."

"Mannering," Harcourt said, sighing. He lay still for a moment and then suddenly the heavy lids of his eyes opened, his hand clutched Mannering's and he actually started up. "Mannering!"

"Yes, I'm here," Mannering said, very clearly. "What can I do?"

"Save her," Harcourt said thickly. "Save Lucille. They will kill her. Or they will ruin her. They say she is mad – but she is not. They say she murdered her husband – but she did not. They hate her. Save—"

He broke off.

For a moment the hand clutching Mannering's kept its grip, then slowly it loosened. The nurse appeared as if from nowhere, gently easing his head back to the pillow.

Harcourt's eyes closed.

"I should think he has said all he wanted to say, Mr. Mannering," said Dr. Medway quietly, "and I hope very much that you will be able to do what he asks. I believe he kept himself alive simply to beg this of you."

It was Medway who now held the stage, a man with both strength and gentleness in his expression.

"I'll do what he wants if I get all the help I need," Mannering said, and before Medway could ask what he meant he went on: "Do you know the Peek family?"

Dr. Medway shook his head.

"Not really. I met Ezra and his wife once at a dinner party, that's all."

"Are. you Mr. Harcourt's regular physician?"

"Yes. I have been for over thirty years."

They were at the door, now. The younger doctor and the nurse were by the patient's side. Barely above a whisper Mannering asked: "What are you going to put on the death certificate?"

"There's only one thing to put," replied Medway. "Death from natural causes. Mr. Harcourt has suffered from heart trouble for at least fifteen years. All stresses, strains and shocks are bad for him, particularly emotional shocks. He is a man who involves himself deeply in his clients' affairs, and identifies with them. This affair has been more than he can stand: it is as simple as that." He shook hands with Mannering, said again: "It was good of you to come," and returned to the sick room. Young Pace stood a little awkwardly by the open door of the lift.

"Would you like to use the lift?"

"May we walk?"

"Yes, of course."

Pace led the way to the stairs while Mannering looked about him. This was a Victorian house both inside and out, he did not see anything of an older period except, perhaps, some landscape paintings. Most of the pictures were portraits of the kind one was likely to find in a London club. Everything was solid and well-polished, the curtains were tapestry or velvet, the carpets Wilton or Axminster. Over the front door was a stained glass fanlight.

"Do you know the Peek family?"

"A little," answered Pace. "Mr. Harcourt was really the one who had dealings with them. But I could introduce them to you if you wish."

"Later," Mannering said. "Thank you. But there is something you can do."

"Anything," said Charles Pace earnestly. "Mr. Harcourt was as much a father as a partner to me. My father died young, Norman brought both my brother Roger and I up, put us into the firm, has been—" He broke off; when he spoke again his voice was stronger and more urgent. "Mr. Mannering! What did you mean by asking what Dr. Medway would put on the death certificate?"

Very deliberately Mannering answered: "I wanted to find out whether he had any suspicion of foul play. Apparently he hasn't. Mr. Pace – I want you to find out the name of everyone on your staff who was in the office from which your partner was telephoning when he collapsed. Whether they were clients, members of the staff, anyone at all. And having done that I would like to know if anyone on that list was also close by when Ezra Peek had his last seizure."

"Good God!" exclaimed Pace.

"Will you do it?"

"Of course. I won't lose any time. There's one name which would appear on both lists which I can tell you right away." When Mannering didn't ask what name it was, Pace volunteered: "Mrs. Lucille Peek."

"Can you be sure there was no one else?" demanded Mannering in a strangled voice.

"Not positive in the absolute sense," replied Charles Pace, "but ninety-nine per cent certain. I should know for sure by this evening – shall I telephone you?"

"I'll be grateful if you will," Mannering said.

But on the way back, with a police escort exactly as before, he felt that was the last telephone call he wanted to hear. He was concentrating on it when he saw the driver of the police car in front wave him down, and then pull into the kerb, just halfway down Putney Hill and within sight of Bristow's house. The driver climbed out and came hurrying back.

"There's a message for you, Mr. Mannering – very urgent. Not to go to Quinn's or your flat, but to St. George's Hospital. Someone on your staff has been badly hurt."

13

'Accident'?

About the time that Mannering was approaching Harcourt's house in Wimbledon, Josh Larraby was leaving by the front door of Quinn's. He could always get in and out by the back door and there was a special key to his apartment and special security precautions at the back, against burglary. Coming home, Larraby usually used his private entrance, going out he loved to walk through the shop. In a way, it was 'his'.

He never forgot the first time he had come into it, soon after Mannering had taken over, a thief freshly released from prison, sentenced because of his love of precious stones and the temptation they created and to which he had given way. He never forgot how Mannering, the last person he expected, had given him a chance to rehabilitate himself: to live with the jewels he so loved, and for which he felt so over-riding a passion, and at the same time to live and conquer the temptation to possess. It was well over twenty years ago and much of that time he had been manager at Quinn's, retiring only when he became too old.

He was now eighty-one, and one of the happiest men alive.

He lived, trusted absolutely, within hand's reach of the wondrous treasures at Quinn's. Occasionally, he was called upon to identify or to date a jewel or a piece of jewellery, for he still stored more knowledge than most men acquired in a lifetime in his head. Mannering and Bristow never hesitated to consult him if they were puzzled. He could walk through this shop whenever he liked, and it was like walking through history. And, perhaps the greatest delight of all, he was occasionally invited by Mannering to take part in a valuation such as that for the Peek Collection. It was sheer joy.

The past few weeks with Mannering had tired him one way and yet refreshed him in another, and he was almost sorry about going away for a rest. But physically, no doubt, he needed one. So he left, walking, carrying just an overnight case for he did not intend to be away for long. He turned out of Hart Row, his heart as near to singing as it could be.

He did not see the small car which drove straight at him.

He was on the pavement; it did not occur to him that he was in danger.

There he was, walking sedately, a conventionally-dressed man in a business suit, and coming towards him were two youths with hair growing down to their shoulders, wrapped up in patched coats, unshaven, unwholesome-looking. He tried to avoid a direct stare, thinking: *Really*! What is the world coming to? But his curiosity got the better of him, and on that instant he saw their expressions change from vacuous listlessness to fear. One of them yelled: "Look out!" and dived into a shop doorway.

The other looked beyond Larraby to see the thing that caused him terror, and he leapt forward, carrying Larraby with him. All of a sudden people were shouting, screaming, as the small car mounted the pavement. Had Larraby still been walking there it would have mown him down. As it was he was several feet away, on his back, the long-haired lout half over him. The car went on, crashing into a plate glass window. The driver flung the door open, sprang out and ran, disappearing in the crowd of traffic. Only a few people noticed him; afterwards, no one was able to describe him clearly.

Mannering leapt out of his car outside the side entrance to St. George's Hospital, as Bill Bristow came hurrying down the steps. So it wasn't Bill. He had never seen such an expression on

Bristow's face: a mixture of rage and anxiety. He was almost afraid to ask: "Who?" And then he did not need to ask for there was only one of the staff who could affect Bristow like this.

He asked gruffly: "Josh?"

"Yes."

"How bad?"

"Touch and go. Head injury."

"How did it happen?"

"John," Bristow said, "someone tried to run him down. A passer-by pushed him out of the way of the car but Josh hit his head on the pavement. It's touch and go," he repeated. "The other poor devil has multiple fractures of the legs – both legs." They were now walking up the steps to the hospital.

"Is Josh conscious?"

"They're operating in half-an-hour," Bristow said. "He's had X-Rays and everything possible is being done. He's alive – but only just."

Bristow gulped.

How it had been arranged Mannering did not know, but they were taken straight to the ward where Josh Larraby was lying. He looked ashen pale, and his eyes were closed; whatever drug they had given him had put him right out. There were nurses round his bed, and a young doctor who, at sight of the two men, came forward.

"Mr. Mannering?"

"Yes," Mannering said, and made himself add: "All I want is for you to save him."

"I know," said the doctor. "I've met him at Quinn's, and – well, I can't promise you anything. With a younger man I'd say he had a very good chance indeed. You don't need telling—"

"You'll do your best."

"Our absolute best," the doctor said. "And now we're about ready to start."

"How long will this take?" Mannering asked.

"It could be as long as two or three hours. I'll see that you're informed the moment we can give an opinion."

Mannering went out, walking blindly, hardly seeing the bare walls, the doors he passed, the visitors, the push-carts, the hospital's personnel. He reached the main hall and felt Bristow gripping his arm like a vice. He allowed himself to be pushed towards a chair, and helped to sit down. *Josh.* He had known him for so long, he was – one of the family. *Family.* Josh. Oh, God. He pressed his hand against his forehead and Bristow asked something he didn't hear. Josh. *Family.* Lorna! He straightened up in sharp alarm, the pain driven away from his eyes momentarily.

"Lorna?" He barked the name.

"I haven't told her," Bristow said. "I thought—"

"She must know."

"I thought you would want to tell her," Bristow said, only to add: "I will, if you like. One of us must."

"Lorna," Mannering said, and after a pause: "I'll tell her. Did they get the driver?"

"No."

"Killer," Mannering said. "Killers at large. Do they know it was an attempt to kill him?"

"It's being handled as if it were attempted murder," Bristow said. "By the same team as the one handling your affairs last night. John, I hate asking this but every senior policeman involved is asking me." When Mannering simply looked at him in silent invitation to go on, the words seemed to spill out of him. "Do you know more than you've told us, John?"

Mannering looked at him as if he did not comprehend.

"What a bloody silly question. *No.* Absolutely no, and that is final."

Bristow looked both alarmed and relieved as he said: "Now take it easy, John. No one's accusing you. I'll tell them, right away. Would you like me to drive you to—"

"I'm perfectly capable of driving," Mannering said, and then jerked: "Thanks."

By the time he had reached his car he knew that he had let fly at Bristow because of his own pent-up emotions. Josh Larraby, so near death; the man who had worked with him for so long, who had spent nearly every moment of estimating the value of the Peek Collection with him.

Only one person, so far as they yet knew, had been close to Ezra Peek and Norman Harcourt at the time of their last and fatal shock.

Lucille *couldn't* be involved in such devilry; in an attack on an old man – a helpless old man.

He found himself grinding his teeth as he started the car, but as he moved into the stream of traffic he regained more self-control, concentrated on his driving and was soon in Piccadilly. Traffic was very heavy this morning. He had to wait for minutes to make the turn off which would take him to Hart Row. He saw a police car in his driving mirror; they were certainly making sure they did not lose him.

But nothing could really protect him, or anyone else if someone meant to kill.

While he was sitting there in the Allard, for instance, someone on the pavement or in a nearby car could shoot him. Throw a hand grenade. Or—

He was getting fanciful!

There was nothing fanciful about this business, it was all happening, and he had to find out why. First the why, and then, who was at the back of it? And it was past time he stopped this emotional brooding, the tensions; he could not concentrate on the vital issues unless he could stand aside and look at them objectively. First why and then who by? It was glaringly obvious that the attacks on him had started only when he had finished the valuation and when he had identified Lucille. The attack – if it had been an attack – on Harcourt had come soon afterwards. So had the attack on Josh; the last, the unforgivable attack.

Why Josh Larraby?

He was driving along Bond Street now and would soon turn off to Hart Row, without realising that he was passing the very spot where Josh had been attacked. The truth of the affair, or at least part of it, came to him with shattering force. He and Josh were both wanted dead *because* they had valued the Collection.

Nonsense?

No: it gave a motive which he hadn't seen before. Someone wanted them dead because of the valuation.

Had he been the only intended victim it could be because he might be able to help Lucille to sell the Collection. Might be able? He would be able. There was no if about it, and if he had to he could borrow against the security of the Collection. Now that Josh was involved it could only be because they had worked together on the Collection and knew it thoroughly, perhaps more thoroughly than any man since Ezra Peek's death.

Now he felt a warning passing through his body – there was something in the Collection itself which was bringing these attacks upon them. Something Harcourt might know, too. He—

There was a traffic block at the corner to Hart Row, and as he sat, waiting now and no longer fuming, turning the new idea over and over in his mind, he suddenly realised that he shouldn't be here: he had left for Chelsea and Lorna, he had spent all this time in the thick of London traffic going in the wrong direction! Fit to drive, was he? He actually laughed, and that in itself showed an improvement; a few minutes before he would just have been mad at himself. What was the best thing to do? If he went to his usual parking place he could walk through the office block to Piccadilly and get a taxi from there – no. Taxis were too risky at rush hour.

He must drive.

He was crawling past the entrance to Hart Row when he saw Charles standing outside the shop looking this way and that. Immediately Charles spotted him he waved and began to run towards him. At that moment the traffic ahead began to move; traffic could be as contrary as people. He was at one side, saw Charles turn the corner in the driving mirror, ignored a taxi behind him, and stopped. Charles reached the window.

"Two things, sir. Mr. Norman Harcourt died this afternoon and – well, the other is that you're to go to Chelsea as quickly as you can, sir. To your flat. I don't know what's the matter but Mrs. Mannering's most anxious."

So now there was trouble with Lorna; *for* Lorna.

He said: "Thanks, Charles. It's touch and go with Josh but he's having the operation now."

He drove into an empty stretch of road and from that moment everything seemed to go his way; he was able to catch the lights of Bond Street and Piccadilly, was soon in St. James's Square. Traffic seemed to divide for him in Pall Mall. He went right at the Mall and swung round Buckingham Palace, towards Victoria, and when he was in Fulham Road saw a police car just behind him. He gave a snort of a laugh: those drivers were incredible! At last he was in King's Road, Chelsea, outside the Town Hall, and it would not be long now.

Why would Lorna send for him so urgently without giving a reason?

Had she heard about Josh?

Charles may have told her, but that would not create an emergency at the Chelsea flat, and Lorna would not cause one unless there was real need. He was forced to slow down a little; and at the same time made himself think of the new motivation. What could Josh and he have discovered or seen in that Collection which would make someone want to kill them?

There had been hundreds of pieces: seven hundred and ninety-one to be exact. Did all of them together or just one of them hold the secret?

Should he be worrying more about Lorna? There were police back and front at the house and he could imagine no reason why she should be in danger, but nevertheless he began to fret. What was holding up the traffic? It started to nose forward and he took a turning to the left, making for a rabbit warren of streets which would lead him to the Embankment and the other end of Green Street. Ah! Now he could move. So could the police car. An elderly man stepped off the kerb outside a pub, and Mannering jammed on his brakes. Careful. He had a vivid mental picture of Josh lying on a narrow hospital bed, pale and still under the anaesthetic.

He turned into Green Street.

Two plainclothes men were still on duty, and neither of them showed any sign of panic or alarm. One of them moved across and asked: "Like me to park your car, sir?"

"Would I!" He climbed out of the door as the other opened it. "Has there been any trouble?"

"*I* haven't seen any, sir." Alarm showed in the man's eyes. "Have you any reason to believe—"

"I'll call down from the window if there's any need," Mannering said over his shoulder as he hurried into the house. The lift was on the ground floor and only half-a-minute elapsed before he was at the door of his own apartment, key in hand. Suddenly, he remembered: *I have to tell her about Josh,* and then he opened the door and stepped inside.

There was no sign of anyone, but he heard Lorna saying: "I'm quite sure he won't be long. He will come the moment he gets the message."

Another woman answered her: "I am frightened in case they kill him. If they do I would never forgive myself. Never."

The voice was Lucille's . . .

14

Fear From Guilt?

They were in the drawing -room, the one formal room in the apartment, which overlooked the street. Although Lorna made changes from time to time basically it was much the same as it had been for many years; a Regency room of golds and greens and pale greys.

Lucille was standing by one of the two windows, and the sun, coming through for the first time that day, glinted on her hair. Lorna was sitting on the arm of a large chair, still in her painting smock, a little dishevelled, obviously concerned. Mannering reached the doorway and watched them. He would never understand how it was that he felt so calm.

Quietly, he said: "Well, they haven't killed me yet."

Lucille sprang round. Lorna stood up, and relief touched her face with sombre beauty. There was a moment of silence, in Lucille it seemed of stupefaction; then suddenly she ran across to him, and there was nothing he could do but cradle her in his arms.

She began to cry.

There was no way at all to find out if it were a genuine paroxysm, or whether she was able to act so well that it seemed so. Her arms were bent in front of her, her head was lowered to his chest, and her whole body shook. He found himself stroking the back of her head with one hand while holding her in the other arm. He looked across at Lorna.

"How long?" he asked.

"Over an hour," Lorna replied.

"Has she been like this all the time?"

"In spasms," Lorna answered, a little drily, "and if you think she's acting, I don't think she is."

"I hope she isn't," Mannering said. "If I thought she was, I—"

"I didn't realise that she had been living on her nerves so much," Lorna said. "It leaves you no alternative but to help her."

"Yes," he said. "If I can and when I'm sure I should."

"What makes you say that?"

He did not answer for a moment, but stilled his hand on the back of Lucille's head, which was bent so that he could see the nape of her neck and the ends of her hair lying in short, half-circular curls. She was still sobbing, but not so loudly, and it was possible that she could hear what he was saying. If there was guilt in her and if this was a fear born of guilt, then he wanted her to hear. If she were innocent then it could do no harm for her to know what he felt.

"Because I'm not sure whether she is partly responsible for what's happening," he said. There was no change in Lucille's movements, nothing to suggest that she heard him. "And I am going to find out who *is* responsible, even if I break their necks with my bare hands."

He waited, but there was no pause in the low-pitched sobbing or the near-convulsive movements of her body.

"John," Lorna said. "What's happened? What's got into you?"

So she didn't know about Josh.

"I hate to have to tell you this," he said, and gave a short, mirthless laugh, "when I haven't even a free arm with which to comfort you, but this morning Josh was attacked and seriously injured. He's in hospital now, and – it's touch and go whether he lives or dies."

Lorna said: "Oh, dear God."

She rose slowly from the arm of her chair and moved towards him. He noticed without giving it much thought, that she limped. She drew nearer and he took his hand away from Lucille's head and held it out to her.

"And it really is—touch and go?"

"I've just come from the hospital."

She drew his arm to her, and it was as if each of them was oblivious of Lucille, whose sobs were less convulsive now and whose body was less tense. This moment when she might indeed be listening, Mannering virtually ignored her.

"But why?" asked Lorna, helplessly. "Why?"

"It must be something to do with the Peek Collection," Mannering said. "We are the only two who have examined every piece, and this persecution didn't start until after we had finished. Josh is in the hospital and will be closely guarded, and in any case he won't be able to talk for some time." The words seemed to force themselves from his lips. "So presumably I am now the only target," he added.

Lorna said: "It's hideous." She released his hand and moved away; this time he was acutely aware that she was limping.

"What's the matter with your leg, darling?"

"Oh, I'm so mad at myself I slipped coming down from the attic. It isn't much but if I put more than a little weight on it—"

"What have you done for it?" asked Mannering.

"Oh, it—"

"Cold water compress," Mannering said, and he wished the elder policeman of the previous night was here, with his expert knowledge on first-aid.

He felt Lucille stir, and took his hand away from her. She sniffed, then dabbed at her eyes and cheeks, forlorn and red-eyed.

"I am sorry," she said. "It is my fault – it happened when I came, I kept my finger on the bell. Now, though, I can help, I am – I *was* – a nurse." She went down on her knees in front of Lorna and took the left foot into her hand. "It is I think a sprain, perhaps it would be best to go into the bathroom." She straightened up and offered her arm to Lorna for support. "John, will you please lead the way?" He found himself obeying, and once in the bathroom, running cold water, putting a stool in position for

Lorna to sit on. "If you have bandages I can make a compress," she said, and looked up. There were tears in her eyes as she went on: "Please let me do something for you."

He gave her what she wanted, then stood watching as she set to work. First she bathed the ankle, and then bound it firmly, resting Lorna's foot on her knee. Then she plunged the foot and ankle into cold water, dried it partially, and pulled on an ankle support. The whole task had taken less than ten minutes, and in those ten minutes much of the tension as well as much of Mannering's anger had eased.

"No, please, do not use the leg any more than you can help. Your very domesticated husband must cook for you. Or else—" Suddenly her eyes danced and she said the last thing Mannering dreamt of hearing. "Or better, perhaps, I come here and look after you both.

You are familiar with the way the great Dumas introduced his women? 'This,' he would say, 'is the wife of my bed! And this,' he would say turning to another, 'is the wife of my kitchen!'" She looked intently at Mannering whose expression had changed. "Oh, please, do not take me so serious, I only joke. I—"

She stopped and turned to Lorna; Mannering, too, looked at his wife. Quite suddenly and uncontrollably she began to laugh.

"John," Lucille said, "you are a very lucky man. Where is the best place for Lorna to rest?"

"The study," Lorna managed to gasp. "Help me there, darling." She fought back another spasm of laughter. "If you could only have seen your face!"

"Obviously he does not think *a ménage à trois* a good idea," Lucille said. In anyone else it would have sounded brazen, but she said it so lightly and matter-of-factly that Mannering found himself near laughter, too. He helped Lorna into a comfortable chair, and then made himself speak sharply: "Lucille, nothing is funny about this."

"I know," she admitted, eyes downcast.

"Why did you come here?"

"To see you – to warn you."

"About more attacks?"

"Of course, what else?" Lucille replied. She sat on a pouffe, one which Lorna often sat on when she and John were alone in the evening. "After you went last night I received telephone calls, and again this morning. A man told me he would not rest until you were dead."

"What man?" Mannering demanded.

She hesitated before saying: "I am not sure."

"Do you think you know?"

"Oh yes, I think I know," admitted Lucille. "But I must not tell you, or you will go and see him and he will kill you."

"Doesn't it occur to you that I might kill him?"

She shook her head. "Most certainly not. If you ever kill a man it will be by accident, but this one – he will kill because he hates, or because someone might get in his way. Am I not right about your husband?" She shot the question at Lorna, but went on before there was time for an answer. "John, I have decided what to do."

"Oh, have you," Mannering said drily.

"Yes. I am going to give the Collection to Ezra's sons. When they have it there will be no more trouble, I am quite sure of that. I will not allow risk to you or to other innocent people." She held her hands out towards him, appealingly. "You will understand, it is mostly for you. If I love you, and this I do, I will not allow bad things to happen." Again she turned to Lorna and asked frankly: "Would *you* allow such things to happen to him?"

"Not if I could avoid it," Lorna answered.

"You see?" Lucille turned back in triumph to Mannering. "I can prevent it, so I do. I want you please to have no more to do with this affair. To allow the sons of my husband to take the Collection, and then – the trouble will be over."

"And you?" asked Lorna.

"I will go away from England," Lucille said quietly. "It would not be good for me to stay here, especially in London. It would not be easy, and John has such a woman for his wife! I will tell you this," she added, turning to Lorna, "I hoped very much I would not like you. I would not mind what I attempted to do if I did not like you. But I like you very much, and I see that John is everything to you. So, John, please —"

"Why did you come here?" demanded Mannering.

"I came to plead with your wife to make you stop working for me."

Lorna said: "That's exactly what she asked me, John."

"And when you could not be found I thought that already you had been killed," went on Lucille. "For some awful minutes I believed you to be dead, it was – it was awful for me, and I could not stand it. These past few months have been so hard, and the one friend I had is now dead, or so near death they do not think he will live one more day."

"Norman Harcourt?"

"Yes," she said, quietly. "It is better I should go, John. Lorna, she will agree with me, won't you Lorna?"

Lorna did not reply immediately. The other woman had simply glanced at her as if assuming her agreement but when Lorna did not speak Lucille frowned and looked at her more intently. Mannering, sure what was in Lorna's mind, dropped into an armchair. He had a headache and was tired, suddenly sick of the whole scene.

Lorna said at last: "No."

"But I do not understand," Lucille protested.

"You don't even begin to understand John if you think he would allow you to do this," Lorna said. "Does she, John?"

"But it is madness! I can go out of your lives. And there will be no danger. There is no other choice." Lucille's eyes flashed, momentarily touched with anger. "Lorna, you cannot mean—"

"I mean these men not only attacked John but tried to kill an old friend, a very old friend," Lorna said. "Neither of us could rest if we just did nothing."

"And you are not afraid of *me*?"

"I am not at all afraid of you," Lorna said gently.

Lucille looked from one to the other as if she could not believe what she was hearing.

"Lucille," Mannering said. "Who do you *think* telephoned you?"

"I—I do not want to tell you."

"I might get badly hurt trying to find out," Mannering said mildly. "Who made you change your mind?"

After a long pause, with her eyes half-closed and her hands clenched, Lucille said: "I do not want you to be killed. Please don't make me tell you."

"If you don't tell me I shall believe you are lying," Mannering said.

"Lying?" she echoed. "Lying? For what reason should I lie? For a little while I think you are the man who will help me, then I fall in love with you – after last night, more, so much more than ever before. Because I know you are a good man, that because a beautiful woman throws herself at your head you do not think only of taking her to bed, you do not think of that at all! Such a man! I do not—"

"Who was the man who telephoned?" demanded Mannering. "Or do you really want me to get impatient?"

He thought she would go on arguing, but something in his expression and perhaps in the intent way in which Lorna was staring at her, made her change her mind. She waved her hands above her head in a gesture of helplessness, then sprang to her feet and cried: "It was George Peek, the eldest son. The one who lives at Ealing."

"And how long has George Peek been a criminal?" demanded Mannering.

"I do not understand. Why do you say he is a criminal?"

"You cannot get four, or even two, assassins to commit murder for you just by snapping your fingers," Mannering said drily. "You must have friends in the trade. Hired killers are not so easy to come by in England even among the criminal classes. So George must be involved in crime, and probably his brother also. Are they? Is that the heart of this matter, Lucille? Are the Peek brothers, and was their father, involved in crime – not just over the Collection but for a long period?" He stood up and put a hand peremptorily on her shoulder. "Is that what Norman Harcourt was trying to tell me?" He stared down into Lucille's golden eyes as he shook her. "Is that why you killed him? Is that what he was really trying to say?"

She did not answer.

He shook her again but she did not answer and she did not try to pull herself free. And it seemed to Mannering at that moment that her actions, her fears, were built out of guilt.

15

Gang Of Thieves

"John," Lorna said into the quiet which followed his questions, "you're hurting her. Let her go."

Mannering did not appear to hear Lorna's appeal. Nor did he shift his grip or change his own bleak and savage expression.

"Come on. Let's have the truth. Is the Peek family just a gang of thieves? Is that Collection stolen? *Tell me!*"

"John, please."

Lucille said explosively: "Yes. All that is true." She seemed, to Lorna, to be a woman who did nothing by half measures. What, she thought in dismay, was going to be revealed *now*? "They are a gang of thieves. All of them. My husband, and his sons. My husband was – I do not know the word you use."

"A fence?"

"That is a man who buys stolen goods?"

"Yes."

"Then that is the word."

"Well, well," Mannering breathed, letting her go. "And you are one of them."

"John!" cried Lorna, "that's enough!"

Again he ignored her, and in those minutes he did not seem to be the man she knew; he was harder, more unyielding, there was nothing that could be reached by appeal. There appeared to be no understanding in him.

"Tell me," he rasped. "You are one of them and you've fallen out. Is that the truth?"

He seemed to see old Norman Harcourt on his death bed pleading with him to help Lucille, saying that 'they' accused her of killing her husband, of being mad. Saying that he feared they would kill her. Had he really believed in her? Could he have lied, knowing he was soon to die? Had he been trying, earlier, to warn Mannering about the family and had something made him change at the last moment?

How could he tell?

Lucille said: "I was his wife. I was under obligation to his sons. Yes, I was one of them. But I did not know then that they were what you call a gang of thieves. Afterwards, yes, I found out, but at the time I did not know. We always hated each other, the sons and I. We pretended to be friends for his sake. This I will say to you: they loved their father. They had great admiration and respect for him. But now – they want everything, they want me to have nothing."

"You have an annuity."

"Oh, I have a little. But—" She turned away from him. "But I tell you the best thing now is for me to agree. I do not want you killed. I do not want your friends killed. It was a bad thing that I asked for your help. If I go now I can make terms – and if you allow them to have the Collection there will be no more trouble." She swung away from Mannering and thrust her arms out towards Lorna. "You make him see sense, please. Please."

"There isn't any way to make him," Lorna said.

"Then he will be killed!"

"He has been in danger before," .Lorna told her. "And now he is fully warned."

"You would let him go out to this danger—"

"I would let him do whatever he thinks is right," Lorna said, and she took one of Lucille's hands in her own. "Come and sit down, and do what you yourself suggested. Stay here until it is all over. I *do* need help and John says you are a superb cook. The house is guarded and probably no one knows you're here. Stay for a while, Lucille." She looked up at her husband. "Isn't that what you think she should do, John?"

"I'm quite sure it is," Mannering said.

"I do not think I shall ever be able to understand you two people," said Lucille. "But – John, will you tell the police all this?"

"Not yet," Mannering said. "What will you do?"

"Among other things have a talk with your stepsons, who—"

He broke off as the telephone bell rang, and for a moment hesitated. Then he stretched out for the extension near him. The fear that sprang to his mind was that this was news of Josh, and if news came so quickly it was almost certain to be bad. He held his breath before giving his name.

"Mannering."

He heard the voice of the man who had spoken to him on the telephone about Lucille; it was so filled with venom and with hate that he could not fail to recognise it – might never be able to forget it.

"John Mannering," the voice said. "I've got news for you. If Lucille doesn't come out of your flat in the next half-an-hour we're going to come and get her. It wouldn't make any difference if you had forty coppers instead of four, they wouldn't be able to stop us. Just send her out."

As Mannering put the receiver down, both Lorna and Lucille looked at him intently. He knew that his expression must have given away the fact that it had been an ugly call. He had to decide quickly what to tell them. If the truth, then he thought Lucille would want to leave at once; if a half-truth, neither of them would be convinced. The sound of the man's voice echoed within his head, '. . . we'll come and get her. It wouldn't make any difference if you had forty coppers. '

That could only be bluff.

Unless 'they' virtually used an army there was no way in which they could break into the flat and get Lucille. And they could not send as many men as that. Did 'We'll come and get her' mean just that, or . . . that wasn't exactly what the man had said, though. 'We're going to come and get her' – that was it. The rest was unimportant.

Both women watched him, but neither asked a question: that in itself was remarkable. Lucille had moved and was standing by Lorna, as if she needed her protection. Should he tell them the truth? No, he couldn't.

He said simply: "More threats."

"What about?" asked Lorna.

"Threats to kill."

"But why should they want to kill you and Josh? Why—" She turned to Lucille and demanded furiously: "Do you know? If you have any idea at all you must tell us. It could make the difference between life and death."

"No," replied Lucille, without hesitation. "Only one thing can make that difference now. John, it is no use being obstinate. You must let me go to them and tell them I will agree, and you must let them have the Collection. Everything else is dangerous and useless." When he made no comment she turned, not on him but on Lorna. "Don't you understand! I *will* do not do this, they will kill him! Don't you care enough for him to sacrifice me – a bad woman, a scarlet woman, a *whore*. Please," she begged. "There is nothing more to do."

Mannering said: "You really want to go away from here, now?"

"Yes. And I want you to stop—"

"Do you know who that was on the telephone just now?

"Perhaps, one of my step-sons."

"Let me tell you exactly what he said," said Mannering, changing his mind with great deliberation. "He said that if you didn't come out of here in the next half-hour he and his friends would come and get you. He—"

"Then I must go!" cried Lucille. She broke free of Lorna and rushed across the room but Mannering caught her. She struggled furiously. "Let me go, it is madness to keep me here! They will do terrible things!"

"Oh, I am going to let you go," Mannering said. "But not quite in the way they expect." Holding her firmly with one arm he moved to the telephone, and with the other lifted the receiver and then dialled a number: Quinn's number. Bristow answered almost at once, and Mannering said quietly: "Bill, I've Lucille Peek at the flat. I think she is playing a part in a conspiracy to defraud, and I think she should be charged and taken into custody. She seems to think that she might be in some danger herself, so I should say three police cars, for safety's sake. Do you think your influence at the Yard is strong enough to make them act quickly?"

"They won't lose a second. Do you seriously think—oh, later!" Bristow banged down the receiver, while Lucille tried again to free herself, though less vigorously. Mannering said gently: "I still don't know what it's all about, Lucille, but I'm sure you'll be safer in a prison cell for a few hours than you will anywhere else in London. It is the one place where they cannot possibly do you any harm."

As if helplessly, Lucille said: "You are making a terrible mistake. Terrible! You will never be able to say that I did not warn you." She sniffed back tears. "Please," she said. "I need a handkerchief."

Mannering let her go, and she moved across to her bag, which was on a chair, took out a handkerchief and blew her nose. There were moments when she could look like a small, dispirited child, and this was one of them. She turned towards Lorna, going behind Mannering, and appealed: "Cannot *you* make him see? Don't you care if—"

Without a second's warning she kicked him in the back of his right knee, and his leg doubled up beneath him. He pitched forward over Lorna, and the chaise longue, while Lucille rushed through the door, slamming it behind her. A second afterwards came the boom of the hall door closing. Mannering, afraid of hurting Lorna, his knee painful, and feeling an utter fool, seemed to take an age to get up. He moved towards the door but stopped, as Lorna said: "She'll be in the street by now – you won't catch her, darling."

"I'm not sure I want to," he said ruefully. He reached a window in time to see Lucille getting into the red M.G. He might stop her by shouting down to the police, but he was genuinely not sure what to do.

Five minutes later, when two policemen arrived from the Division, he said: "The moment she knew what I planned, she panicked. And all I wanted was her own safety.

On the whole the police, including the Divisional superintendent to whom he spoke on the telephone, took the situation well.

"What are you going to do now?" Lorna asked.

"Just as soon as I can I'm going to see George Peek," answered Mannering. "I don't think there is any other way of finding out what it's all about."

Lorna said drily: "Well, one thing is certain. She seems very devoted to you."

"Well, if she is, I wish she weren't."

"You shouldn't wish that," Lorna said, with more than a shade of amusement. "I quite like her."

He didn't speak.

"There is a kind of honesty about her—"

"Honesty? Perhaps so, and perhaps not, but if so, after what she has told us, it's certainly a peculiar variety," said Mannering. "I wish I knew for certain whose side she's on and just what she's up to. I wish I knew whether she ran away for my sweet sake or whether she was terrified of going to prison. She may be honest in one sense – even criminals can be that – but whether she's honest as the law understands honesty I wouldn't like to say."

"I think she's prepared to make any sacrifice for you," Lorna said, as if everything could be forgiven for that.

"Possibly," Mannering said, "but I had to make sure she couldn't. I would hate to think she had been martyred trying to save my life."

"Well, what *are* you going to do?" Lorna asked.

"First, ask the police to send a policewoman here to look after you. Second, change my appearance somewhat. Three, visit this George Peek on his home ground."

He stretched out his hands to help her to her feet, and as she started to get up the telephone bell rang. He thought: that man's ringing again, let him wait. He helped Lorna to a chair, and then lifted the receiver.

"Mannering," he said crisply.

"Mr. Mannering," a woman said briskly. "Mr. Stephens of St. George's Hospital would like a word with you."

"I'll hold on," Mannering said, and covering the mouthpiece whispered to Lorna: "It's news of Josh."

News, beyond doubt; it was agony waiting to find out whether it was good or bad. And the waiting dragged on for a long time, until suddenly a man spoke briskly: "Mr. Mannering . . . I promised to let you know how Mr. Larraby came through the operation. I'm happy to say he came through very well, and while there are obvious dangers to a man of his age, there is no damage to the brain tissues and given average luck he will pull through . . . By all means call whenever you wish, and ask for Surgical B. Goodbye." He rang off before Mannering could say another word.

Lorna, seeing his face, cried happily: "He *will* be all right!"

"He came through well," Mannering said. "Very well." He replaced the receiver slowly as he went on: "I wonder if the same will be said of Lucille."

Lorna's smile faded. "And you," she said, "You could be in danger too."

"Ah," breathed Mannering, very softly. "But I'm going to disappear."

He meant just that. He would go upstairs to the attic, and by the use of some highly specialised disguise techniques within half-an-hour no one would recognise him. He would go from this house across the roof to the house next door and leave from there; no one would give him a second thought. For years he had practised this disguise, until by now it was near perfection. She was quite sure that when he came down to say goodbye it would be like looking at a stranger.

It was.

He wore different clothes, looked fatter because of the bulky inner-lining of the suit, had clipped his hair making his face look plumper. He had even managed to change the size of his eyes by glueing them at the corners; altered the shape of his nose by using wax, put lines on his face.

She knew what he was carrying round his waist, too; a complete set of burglar's tools, some nylon rope, a kind of grappling iron, another, larger tear-gas pistol and a small automatic which would kill at thirty yards. She did not make a fuss when he left, after asking for police protection here, but she watched from the big room window and saw him walking towards King's Road. None of the police appeared to take more than a casual notice of him.

He turned the corner . . .

Even before then he had become a different man; not only different in appearance but in outlook. It was back in the days, long ago, when he had pitted his wits against the police and public over and over again; when he had trained himself to force any lock, break into any strong-room, escape from anywhere which threatened him.

He had been so much younger then, but he had a much greater purpose, now.

Apart from Lorna the only person who even suspected what he planned to do was Bristow and Bristow was glad that he only suspected and could not prove that John Mannering, alias Jonathan Mason would break into George Peek's Ealing house before the day was out.

16

The House At Ealing

Mannering needed a little time to 'live' the part.

He reached a bus stop on the other side of King's Road, waited in the cold, clear evening for ten minutes, until a bus came along, like a huge red monster. It was half-empty, and a Pakistani conductor was sitting on one of the seats near the door.

"You go top deck, sir?"

"No. Inside," Mannering said.

"Where you go, sir?"

"Putney Bridge," Mannering said, and paid his fare. The Pakistani clanged the ticket machine like a child playing with a new toy, smiling broadly as he did so. Mannering accepted the ticket absent-mindedly, still going over the events of the day, and still asking the key question: could Lucille be trusted? The sudden warmth in the relationship between her and Lorna was astonishing, and yet, was anything a woman did astonishing?

Had Lucille really run away to 'save' him?

Or was she playing some deep game which so far he had not begun to understand? If so, the inconsistencies in what she had said and done were easier to explain; but then, extreme nervous tension could explain the inconsistencies, too. If he had to bet he would bet on her goodwill, but if he had to stake his life that would be a hundred times more difficult to decide.

He got off the bus at the stop before the bridge, near a side street which led to a line of small factories and garages. Under the name, and in the character of Mason, he rented a garage on the premises of one of the factories, and it opened straight onto the street. He had rented similar garages within easy reach of Green Street, but had been forced to change them several times.

This one had cement block walls and a metal rollover doorway, and was well-lit with fluorescent lighting. He unlocked and pushed up the door; there was a small, dilapidated Morris inside, the kind of car no one would notice. He switched on the light, checked the car, and his make-up, then switched off the light and drove out, closing the door before he started back along New King's Road.

He parked the car under a group of trees near Parsons Green, and walked across the road to a pub which had been there for as long as he could remember. Only half-a-dozen or so people were in it. Propped up in the bar was a chalked notice: *Tonight: Special: Cottage Pie, 2 Veg, Ginger Pudding.* He ordered a meal, and sat at a table with half-a-pint of bitter until it was ready. He knew the food here well, and considered it to be as good, if not better, than nine out often that he would get in a West End restaurant.

It was after seven o'clock when he had finished.

He drove away, first to Hammersmith and then to Chiswick. At the traffic circle approaching the M4 and the Great West Road he turned towards Hanger Lane, and soon found himself at Ealing Common. He pulled in, off the main road, and studied a map of London he kept in the car. In a few moments he had pinpointed Cirencester Street. He was within half-a-mile of it, had only to drive across the Common and turn along one of the many streets of residential houses.

What *had* Norman Harcourt wanted to tell him?

Had his heart attack been induced? And if it had, and could be proved that it had, then the odds on Ezra Peek having been murdered were much higher. He drove on, and as he reached the cross-roads a patch of mist appeared, causing drivers to jam on their brakes.

He stopped.

In one way fog would help him; in another it could hinder a quick getaway.

He decided that on the whole it would help, because he had not come to take anything from here, only to find out what he could. Unless he found Lucille . . .

His heart began to beat faster.

The traffic eased forward as the fog thinned, but now all the distant lights were misted; one side of the Common was crystal clear, at the other, driving was a tricky business. At least he knew exactly where he wanted to go, took the turnings shown on the map and then ran into a thick patch of fog. Hearing people walking by, he pulled down the far side window and called: "Can you help me, please?"

A pair of youths loomed out of the fog.

"I'm looking for Cirencester Street, I wonder if you know—"

"You're practically in Cirencester Street," one of the youths said. "Keep close to this kerb and when it swings left that's the beginning."

"Thank you." Mannering spoke in the manner of a fussy old man. "Thank you indeed."

A few yards along the night was clearer and he saw a sign on the fence outside a house, reading Cirencester Street and just beyond, the numeral 2. So he was on the right side of the road; everything so far was going his way. A few cars were parked, but their red lamps were easily seen. He found Number 20, pulled in behind a larger car, and got out. It was misty here, and on foot the night seemed strangely eerie. The stars were hidden, there was huge haloes round the tall, old-fashioned street lamps. He was between two of these when he came to The Elms. The gate stood wide open. Lights shone from the front door, through glass panels, and at two upstairs windows. Fearful of making too much sound, he stepped from the gravel driveway on to the grass. Moisture from shrubbery brushed his arm as he passed.

The driveway led off at the left-hand side of the house, and a white sports car was parked at one side.

He walked round it to the back door – and saw the shape of

garages beyond; there were three. He went closer. All three doors were open and in each garage was a car. He felt the radiators. Two were warm, the third was cold enough to show that one car at least hadn't been used for some time.

He went out again and made a complete circuit of the house. All the ground floor windows were shut, but two on the first floor were open, one of them close to the back porch. He would have no difficulty getting in. He went round again, making himself familiar with the windows and doors. On the far side heavy curtains blotted out light except in a pale glow at the edges, and he judged this to be near the kitchen, which was brightly lit although Venetian blinds were down. The curtained room was probably the dining-room.

He began to feel cold in the night air.

Just for a moment, he hesitated; John Mannering of today took over from the Baron of the past: that Baron would not have hesitated for a second. He overcame the hesitation and moved to the back porch. There were ledges in the wall in the corner, many of these Victorian houses might have been made for burglars.

He worked on thin cotton gloves to give himself a grip, then pulled himself up to the porch. He made hardly a sound although he was breathing heavily when he reached the top, and paused to get his breath back.

The open window was on the right, and within hand's reach. There was a ledge above and below it, and he pressed close to the wall until he could stand on the lower ledge and grab the top one. Slowly, he shifted his weight from the porch to the ledge, and soon he was crouching on it, one arm inside the room. He pressed down slightly and the window moved easily and without noise. There was enough light to show that only a small table stood by the window, and he could haul himself up on the top ledge, thrust his legs through the open space, turn, and simply step down into the room.

Very carefully, he did all of these things. Soon, he was standing inside the house.

He heard no sound; he made no sound, except for heavy

breathing. He must wait here until he was able to breathe silently. The outline of a door showed against a lighted passage beyond, and gradually he made out the shape of a bed, a wardrobe, oddments of furniture. Slowly, he crossed the room until he reached the door, groped for the handle, and gripped it. He turned it slowly and pulled, a brighter light slowly infiltrating from the passage.

The door was now open enough for him to slip through, and he studied the layout of the first floor.

A narrow staircase to the right was obviously for the use of the staff. The landing itself extended through an archway to the main staircase. There were doors on either side, all shut.

A whirring sound broke the silence, making Mannering's heart jump; a moment later a grandfather clock struck below, eight lingering strokes. As the echoes faded the silence seemed more intense. He turned from the main landing and went up the stairs leading to the servants' quarters; above was a narrow passage, lit from a single electric lamp. In all there were four doors and a loft ladder, leading to what he was sure would be the attic. He went up this quickly, pushed up the hatch cover, and listened; there was no sound. He took a pencil torch from his pocket and shone it about until he found two electric switches. He pressed one down, and a light came on, a naked bulb hanging from a beam. Another light on the other side came on when he touched the second switch.

The air was clean and fresh, showing that the place was well ventilated, and probably used.

He moved towards a gabled window. By now he had lost his sense of direction but when he reached it he saw the street lamps, evidence that it overlooked the front of the house. Outside the fog had thickened, the light through it diffused and ghostly. He tried out the window a fraction: it worked on a hinge and opened upwards. He went back, fully satisfied. One way of escape was assured.

He tried two of the four doors. One was a boxroom packed with trunks and suitcases and a few old pieces of bric-a-brac. The next was a double bedroom, with a woman's negligee flung over a chair. The third door opened onto a bathroom, and the fourth was locked.

He took out a skeleton key and inserted it in the old-fashioned lock, twisted slowly and cautiously and felt the lock click; when it turned full circle the noise seemed very loud. He stood to one side pressing against the wall, but no sound of answering alarm or investigation followed.

He waited a full minute and then pushed the door open, listening intently; and now he could hear the sound of breathing; very soft, very even, but unmistakable. It came from the right. The light was so bad that he could not see a bed or anything else, so he used his pencil torch aiming it low, and half-covering it with his fingers.

This was a bedroom and the bed was behind the door. He saw a woman's legs, and feet; she was not wearing shoes. His heart began to beat faster as he stepped further, into the room, half-closing the door. The light spread slowly and cautiously over the woman on the bed. She was fully dressed, and there was a belt or strap tied round her waist securing her to the bed.

He had found Lucille.

He went closer to her and touched her shoulder but she did not stir. He uncovered the torch to make the light brighter, and raised one eyelid with his thumb. She still did not move but he could see the pin-point pupil and knew that she was unconscious from one of the morphine group of drugs.

And there was no way of telling how long she would remain unconscious.

Slowly, Mannering drew back.

The obvious thing, the only thing surely, was to take her away before he went through the rest of the house.

But how could he get her out?

And even if he was successful in this, what could he do with her when he had her outside?

He could not simply leave her in the car, for he would have to break in again, and on such a night as this she would perish of cold.

He might telephone Bristow, but this was not a venture Bristow should be involved in.

The attic?

He remembered the big trunks, the oddments of furniture. If he took her up there surely she would be safe enough, and if he were forced to talk he could tell George that he had taken her out of the house. He rested the torch on a bedside table and then bent over the bed, groping for the end of the strap. He found it, and it unfastened easily. He left it under the bed and then lifted Lucille and carried her to the doorway.

She was no weight worth speaking of, but – she was worth that weight in gold. She had come, knowingly, to danger; she had come away to draw the danger from him.

No one was in sight; there was still no sound.

He took her up into the attic, put on one of the lights, went towards some hot water pipes, and then rested her on a piece of spare carpeting. Next, he drew two of the trunks in front of her, so that no one glancing that way could see anything to make him suspicious. Satisfied, he went back to her room, pulled the door to and locked it with the skeleton key; the most anyone was likely to do if they were searching for an intruder would be to try the door. If they came to see Lucille – but that was needless worry, they must know that she would be unconscious for several more hours.

He went down the narrow staircase and as he reached the first landing a door downstairs opened, he heard men talking, heard them moving about in the hall. There were three men as far as he could judge. One had a deep, near-guttural voice; one had a high-pitched voice with a curious kind of twang in it, a hint of viciousness: that was the man who had twice called him on the telephone.

The third voice was a pleasant one, undoubtedly English public school; and he had heard it before today.

This was Charles Pace, of Harcourt, Pace and Pace.

17

Three Less One . . .

The man with the guttural voice was saying: "Are you sure you won't have a brandy?"

"No thanks," said Pace. "My family will be expecting me."

"Families can wait," said the harsh-voiced man, with a laugh. "We'll let you go in twenty minutes."

"Well—"

"That's better," said the man with the vicious tone to his voice. "We wouldn't like you to go without drinking to our success, would we, George?"

"It isn't that—" Pace began, and he sounded nervous.

"You bet your sweet life it isn't," said George.

Mannering was now close to the balustrade which ran about the landing, and by bending low could see without being seen. There was nothing surprising about his foreshortened view except perhaps that Pace was between the others and each man was holding one of his arms; it was almost as if they were keeping him prisoner.

The man George was broad and bull-chested, with a short neck. He had close-cut iron-grey hair which would have been luxurious had he let it grow. The hand which held Pace's arm was big, with long, thick fingers. He moved with ease and assurance and spoke clearly despite the cigar which jutted out of the corner of his mouth.

The third man was much taller than Mannering had expected, tall and thin, and from this angle good-looking. His grip seemed to hold Pace more tightly than his brother. He wore a suit of conventional grey, and his hair was pale, wavy and silky-looking.

They reached an open door on the other side of the hall from the room they had left, and as George went in, he said: "We just want to make sure nothing goes wrong, Charles."

"Oh, it won't go wrong, I assure you!"

"I've a few questions to ask and I didn't want the Gordons to hear," George said. "They'll go as soon as they've served coffee."

All three disappeared into the room.

Mannering waited until he heard footsteps, and a man appeared carrying a silver tray; a woman followed him carrying a smaller tray, with a coffee pot, sugar and cream on it. They were middle-aged, and quite unremarkable. They entered and left the room very quietly, and presently Mannering heard the closing of a door.

Moving without any self-consciousness, he went down the stairs. He limped a little, as he always did when wearing disguise, thinking himself into the part of 'Mason', a character he had played so often. He crossed the hall, studying the layout as he did so. There was another door close to the one where the men were, and he opened this: he could slip in there when he heard the others coming.

He could hear voices but could not distinguish the words, so he placed his gloved hands on the handle and turned it very slowly. It was a risk, but it had to be taken. He pushed the door open half-an-inch, in time to hear Pace speak and to confirm what he had already suspected: the partner of the late Norman Harcourt was a frightened man.

"You know perfectly well that I won't let you down," he said.

"There's just one thing that worries me," said George. He turned to his brother. "How about you, Stanley?"

"I've no idea what you mean!" exclaimed Pace.

"Then let me explain," Stanley said in that unpleasant voice that held both sneer and menace. "You had a lot to say to

Mannering when he was at old Harcourt's house this morning, and you seemed very pally. Keep away from Mannering."

"I can't avoid him if Lucille—"

"Lucille won't brief Mannering any more, he's out," declared Stanley Peek with satisfaction.

"What did he want to know?" demanded George.

There was a momentary pause before Pace answered with what seemed to be bewilderment in his voice. "He wanted to know who had been nearby when your father suffered from his fatal seizure, and also when Mr. Harcourt was taken ill at the office. He seemed to think . . . " Pace paused, and George rasped almost without waiting: "Go on! What did he seem to think – or rather, what do you assume he seemed to think?"

"That someone caused the two seizures," answered Pace, still sounding bewildered. "I don't see how anyone with the slightest knowledge of medicine could think that—"

"Did he *say* that's what he meant?" asked Stanley sharply.

"Not in so many words, but—"

"What did you say to him?" demanded George.

"I—I promised I'd try to find out if anyone had been handy at both times and places. I said Lucille had, of course—"

"You said *what*?" roared George.

"I told him Lucille had been present, but—"

George Peek began to laugh, a deep-throated laugh which had something unpleasant about it; while Stanley's high-pitched giggle added a note that was almost obscene. The laughter went on for some time, while Mannering noted two things.

First, someone who had been present at Harcourt's Wimbledon home that day had made a report about what had happened to these men. And second, that for a few moments they had been alarmed, had been fearful that Pace would name someone else who had been present on both occasions. There was a third thing, easy to infer: there *was* a possibility of the attacks being induced, and by the relief in their laughter at the naming of Lucille, it was almost conclusive that she was not the one involved.

Then, who was?

Someone who had been at Harcourt's house?

Slowly the laughing slackened, and the two Peek brothers began to talk again, but the menace had gone from their voices; they were obviously intent, now, on putting Pace at his ease. Pace said very little.

"So you just go on acting as you are and everything will be fine," said George. "You won't have a thing to worry about."

"Not a thing," agreed Stanley, and after a pause he asked: "Did your dear departed partner tell you he had ever been to our cellars?"

Cellars?

"No," answered Pace.

Cellars? wondered Mannering.

"That's good." A brief laugh broke into George's voice again. "So you go on representing Lucille but you do what we tell you and you'll be well paid. Don't do anything without consulting us. If you do—"

"He can say that his partner had grave doubts about Lucille's sanity, surely," Stanley interrupted.

"Oh, sure, sure. That will be okay. But nothing about the other: we want that for the last minute if we have any trouble with the bitch. Well, you said you wanted to go early, Charley boy . . ."

Mannering slipped into the next-door room. The other three appeared in the hall, visible for a second, Pace still in the middle. The front door opened and George exclaimed: "My Gawd, it's getting thick! Sure you won't stay the night, Charley?"

"Oh, I shall be all right!"

There were 'goodnights' before the front door closed and one of the Peek brothers locked it; judging from the sounds he also bolted and chained it. Mannering kept very still. The men walked towards the room from which they had just come but did not go in at once. The roar of a car engine could be heard starting up.

"Shall we go and see Lucille?" Stanley demanded.

"We don't need to worry about her until it's time for her next dose," declared George. "Did you take Pace at his face value?"

"Boy, was that man scared!"

"Yes, I think he was scared all right," George said with obvious satisfaction. "And Mannering's scared, too, or he wouldn't have let Lucille go. We've got them where we want them, Stanley."

"George," Stanley said ruminatively, "I'm not so sure about Mannering. I'm not so sure he's scared.

And I don't like to think of him running around with the idea that someone helped Ezra and Harcourt on their way out."

"There's no chance of proving—"

"I don't like it," Stanley insisted, and for the first time it occurred to Mannering that he was the more formidable of the two brothers." If he talks too much—"

"There's no need to worry, I tell you," George insisted. "Pace will tell him there was only Lucille! Forget it."

"I'm not sure we shouldn't finish Mannering off," Stanley said.

"He's surrounded by police, and followed wherever he goes," George replied. "We have to leave him for the time being. If we want to fix Mannering we can use Lucille. She'll be more amenable when she comes round." His voice held a note of jubilance. "It's all over bar the shouting, I tell you. We got Lucille back, the old boy's dead, Pace is in our pocket – why, even Mannering gave us a hell of a lot of help. We don't need him dead now, Stanley. We've got everything we wanted – yes, sir. We've got our cake *and* we've eaten it!"

He went off into a paroxysm of laughter, and almost immediately Stanley's high-pitched, obscene note joined in.

It was hard to imagine anyone being more pleased with themselves.

There was an awkward silence after their hilarity, broken by George saying: "Why don't we go and have a game of snooker?"

"Good idea," his brother declared and they walked to a room at the far end of the passage. Soon, Mannering could hear the sharp click of the billiard balls as the two men began to warm up for their game.

They would probably be playing for some time: certainly all

the time Mannering needed to look for the cellar.

It might be approached from a cupboard under the stairs; but it was not.

Trusting that the Gordons would still be in the domestic quarters, Mannering searched the ground floor thoroughly but found no possible entrance. He pushed open a door which yielded at a touch and he found himself in a stone passage which obviously led to a brightly-lit kitchen. He heaved a sigh of relief as the blaring sound of radio or television came to him. Now he could move about more freely.

He tried several doors but they led only into storerooms.

He found another passage and an outside door which was locked from the inside. He turned the key, opened it, and saw fog swirling about a lamp over the door. He stepped into a narrow outside passage, found a washroom and an old-fashioned laundry room with a boiler. He was about to leave when he thought he saw the faint outline of a door behind the boiler – the wall there seemed to have been bricked in. He looked again, but could not find the slight division which had attracted his attention. He stood, baffled. Then he began to turn his lamp this way and that. Suddenly he exclaimed: "Ah!"

The outline showed when his torchlight touched it at a certain angle; but for that he would have missed it. He put on the light in the wash-house and studied the wall very closely. There had been a doorway and it was bricked up.

Why?

He moved again to the other side of the boiler, and it occurred to him that there was something very odd about it. The house itself had been modernised without sparing any expense but here was an old-fashioned clothes boiler, much larger than most and converted from gas – he could see the old pipes – to electricity.

Now I wonder, he said to himself, as he studied the 'On' and 'Off' switch. At the first a red light glowed, at the second it went out. He looked inside the boiler and saw the usual circular heating elements. There was a little water inside. It was clear as far as he could judge, with none of the astringent odour one might expect from a boiler in which soda or detergents were often used.

Nor were there any cartons of detergent or soap powders on nearby shelves.

"Well, well," he said aloud, and then began to press or pull everything which might be a switch, but nothing happened until he pressed the On and the Off switches simultaneously. Instantly there was a click, and almost at once the whole boiler began to move, taking one of the stone slabs of the floor with it. Mannering drew back and saw a hole gradually widening, and beyond the hole a flight of brick steps. He felt a surge of excitement at this discovery. The steps appeared to go down at least twenty feet. There was a handrail down one side, and the air was fresh enough to indicate that the cellar was well ventilated.

He switched off the light and went outside, for there was an obvious possibility that the secret opening of the entrance would raise an alarm, but no one appeared; the only lights were those which had shown before. The fog seemed thicker in this small area, and he heard the low-pitched growling note of car engines crawling along in the streets.

He went back to the wash-house and put on the light, then bent down to examine the hole in the floor. On one side were electric switches and when he pressed them a light went on. He went slowly down the stairs, holding onto the rail. At the foot was a steel door, right across his path, and for the first time he wondered whether he could get to the other side. At least one thing was certain, now: this cellar was protected almost as well as his own strong-room at Quinn's. He drew back, studying the door. There was no padlock and no lock that he could see, this was an electrically or an electronically controlled sliding door.

It might be possible to cut through it, but it would take him an age to get the necessary oxy-acetylene cutter – a lightweight one he had used at one time without difficulty. It was possible that this door was controlled by some switch upstairs, but he had no reason to think so; all controls so far had been on the spot.

He began to press the door itself inch by inch, and had reached a ridge which appeared to connect two panels when he felt something give, sought the spot again and pressed for a second time.

Very slowly, the door began to open.

He never knew why he side-stepped suddenly, darting behind part of the door which was still moving. He had hardly reached cover before there was a sharp *zutt!* of sound, a flash – and a bullet honed along the passage and struck the brick steps, sending chippings in all directions.

18

"The Cake"

Mannering stood in the silence of the cellar as the echoes of the shot and the falling pieces of brick stopped. Had he been directly in the opening, the bullet would have caught him in the chest, and by now he would have been dead, or at best, seriously injured.

He stood without moving for some time, partly from shock, and partly to find out if the shot, or the opening of the door, had set off an alarm in the house. The door had appeared to open normally, and had probably caused no trouble. The shot—

He could still hear it, in his imagination.

He did not even have to turn his head to see how big a piece had been chipped out of the steps. But gradually the blood began to warm in his veins and at last he moved. He did so with the greatest caution, for there might be a double barrel, or even a second gun. He peered round the edge of the door. There was the gun, a rifle, propped up against a Y-shaped piece of wood and secured to the ceiling by a taut rope. He could see how the trigger had been wired, so that if the door opened the shot was fired. There must be another press button which would disconnect wire and trigger.

A smell of cordite hung in the air.

He went forward, edging past the gun; and when he was on the other side he lifted the stock from the Y-shaped support and unfastened the nylon rope which was fastened at the top to a hook in the ceiling. He placed the rifle on the floor, behind the door which had slid back beyond the inside wall.

It was one of the oldest tricks; his previous experience of it, his awareness of what could happen must have warned his subconscious and made him leap to one side. He was hot, now; sweating; and his hands felt clammy. He listened intently but heard no sound, yet was sufficiently on edge to go up the stairs and into the wash-house and outside. Except that the fog seemed thicker, everything was the same. He went back to the cellar, keeping to one side of the damaged step, and then moving beyond a kind of air-lock protection of two brick walls, each a little more than half the width of the passage, and each from a different side. The result was to make him go slowly into the cellar beyond, a little nervous as to what these delaying tactics might mean.

He was now in a big room, and the light from behind him showed shelves and shadowed shapes standing on them. He found a switch on the inside of the second half-wall, and fluorescent light flickered for a few moments and then came on brightly. There was not one but four big fluorescent tubes and the room was large enough to need them all. He could see now that the lowest shelf was about a foot from the floor and perhaps two feet wide; the one above, eighteen inches higher and not quite so wide; shelves, in fact, in staggered widths so that there was ample room for the things stored on them.

To Mannering, it was as if he was suddenly back in his own strong-room, for he had seen these *objets d'art* there. He recognised not just one or two but dozens.

There were some ivory carvings of a seated King and Queen, beyond doubt the same; there were statuettes, gem-encrusted knives and vases – a dazzlingly beautiful collection – here. Not at Quinn's, but *here*.

After the first shock he moved towards the nearest, the King and Queen. And as he approached he realised that they were not the same. For one thing the yellowed ivory had been yellowed by some artificial process, not by age. On the Queen's right ear there should have been the tiniest of chips; it wasn't there. It was a beautiful piece of carving; carving in the Far East was one of the crafts which by some miracle had survived; but there was no antiquity, and it was the antiquity which gave the pair their unique value.

He examined other pieces.

There was a jewelled sword, the original of which had a pearl-encrusted handle. The piece at Quinn's had real pearls of great age; there could be no doubt of their rare lustre. But these were cultured pearls, beautiful in their way, but lacking the value of uniqueness and antiquity.

Every piece he examined was a copy; many of them brilliantly executed and lovely in their own right, but – copies.

He fancied he could hear George Peek's voice in his ears: "We've got our cake *and* we've eaten it!"

Here at least was a partial explanation; perhaps the key to it all. The whole of the Peek Collection, itself absolutely genuine, had a replica here; and if the replicas were sold under the guarantee of Mannering's valuation, then they would fetch ten or twenty times their real value. Not just one or two pieces, but all of them. Could he be sure these were 'all' he asked himself. There were so many that there seemed no reasonable doubt. If George and Stanley had their way then they would get the genuine pieces from Lucille and sell the false ones. "We've got our cake *and* we've eaten it!"

He wandered along shelf after shelf, touching pieces which he could almost swear were identical with those at Quinn's, until he reached the end of the cellar. It was so still that he could hear his own breathing. Slowly, he turned back to the shelves and began to examine the walls beyond. There might be a way out from this end, an escape route for an emergency. He could see no evidence, but then it had been almost by accident that he had discovered the real nature of the clothes boiler.

Did a second entrance matter?

He could go upstairs and lock the door to the wash-house,

even if someone stirred abroad they would notice nothing, and no one was likely to venture out on such a night as this. The obvious was the thing to do. He began to walk towards the open door, still bemused, yet trying to come to a decision. One thing dawned on him belatedly. There was no crime in making replicas of *objets d'art* which one owned oneself; no crime unless one tried to pass them off as the real thing. He could not swear that any of the goods had been stolen, and those at Quinn's had come from old Ezra Peek; neither of his sons could be accused of stealing them, even if they had in fact been stolen.

What charge could be levelled against the Peek brothers?

The attacks on him would be enough, but there was no evidence at all that the assailants had been employed by them, unless the voice of Stanley could be called evidence. And that wasn't enough. Tones of voice, nuances, implications, these things weren't evidence: he *had* no evidence yet, all he had were indications that the conditions for a several million pound fraud were in this cellar.

He reached the door and stepped through, stood on the outside and pressed the spot which he had pressed before – and the door began to close. Now that he had finished the main part of his task he began to sweat again. There had been a period when he would have taken success for granted, but this one had gone so smoothly it was like a miracle.

He need not go back into the house.

Needn't he? What about Lucille? He simply hadn't the evidence he needed to send for the police, and if the brothers found her missing they would be bound to search; now he could not argue with himself any longer, he had to get her away.

He reached the back door – and a woman's voice sounded almost in his ear!

"I'll just see if they want anything."

He heard her footsteps inside the house, and the temptation to turn and hurry to his car became almost overwhelming. Stoically he stayed where he was, but the November cold had crept into his bones before the woman's voice sounded again: "No, we can go up now. I've got the coffee things."

'Going up' could only mean up to bed; up to the floor where Lucille had been, up to the floor where he wanted to go.

Would they wash the coffee cups up tonight?

He opened and closed the door quickly and went in; the television or radio was still blaring loudly, and under its cover he crept up the back staircase and on to the attic. In sudden panic he moved the trunks aside; but Lucille was still there, still inert and apparently lifeless under the influence of the drug.

He lifted her over his left shoulder, fireman fashion, and began to go down the top ladder, hearing no voices or footsteps. He was on the landing when a door closed and a woman said: "Are you coming or aren't you?"

Mannering stayed close to the wall at the foot of the ladder, saw the woman coming up; she carried newspapers and books. Her husband followed, carrying a tray with teapot and cups, everything wanted for early morning tea. He was yawning widely and without restraint. The woman, went into the bedroom and switched on the light. If the man so much as glanced up he could not fail to see Mannering.

He turned into the room.

"It's cold up here, we ought to have another heater," the woman said irritably. She closed the door and on the instant Mannering started down the stairs. There was no reason at all to believe either of the brothers would come to the domestic quarters and he should be outside the house in ten minutes, now: seconds. He had reached the main landing when a door opened and George Peek called out: "Now I'm going to tuck Lucille up for the night!"

He began to leap, two at a time, up the main stairs.

Mannering could either cower there with Lucille still over his shoulder, or go forward. And it did not take him a split second to decide what to do. He tightened his grip round Lucille's legs and moved forward. George, halfway up the stairs, did not see Mannering on the landing until he was several steps below.

Then, one foot raised, he grabbed the banisters and came to a startled halt.

Mannering simply shot out a foot and caught the man on the chest. George's fingers slid off the handrail and he toppled backwards, a cry strangled in his throat. As his victim toppled, Mannering turned and strode towards the back staircase. If he ran, he might trip and undo all the good he had done. He heard Stanley cry out but heard nothing from George, except the thudding on the stairs as the big man fell.

"George!" Stanley screamed. "George!"

Mannering reached the passage which led to the kitchen and the back door; the dim light was still on. He saw that the door was both bolted and chained, and shifting Lucille to a more comfortable position, he undid both of these, opened the door and strode outside. Lucille was safe, he was safe: then suddenly he checked. A man appeared at the end of the passage, which led to the garages.

Mannering stood utterly dumbfounded.

He should have known this must be one of George's hired assassins. With the fog swirling about him, an automatic pistol in his hand, he was levelling it at Mannering; or rather, at 'Mason', the character he had assumed. In the seconds which followed it came instantly to Mannering that the other man was just as surprised at the apparition in front of him as he, Mannering, was surprised.

Then, he recognised the other man: it was Charles Pace.

To Pace, he was a stranger in his present guise.

And Pace was working with the Peeks.

He, Mannering, could run; with Lucille over his shoulders there was a chance that the man would not shoot. But he did not know the way in the fog, while running he might stumble. The moments of indecision were swift, but they seemed to drag before Pace said: "Who are you?"

He came nearer and then apparently realised that Mannering was carrying a woman over his shoulder, for he cried: "Who is that?—*don't move.*"

In the voice of 'Mr. Mason' Mannering said: "I'm not going to move with a gun pointed at my belly. This is Lucille Peek."

"What the devil—"

Mannering said: "Why did you come back? You were in the house with them, I heard you talking. What are you doing here?"

"I came to—" Pace broke off. "That's my business. Who—?"

"I work for Mannering," Mannering said roughly. "He wanted to find out if Mrs. Peek was here and told me to get her away if I could." He moved a step forward, and Pace did not threaten again. "They had kidnapped her. They're killers, I hope you know what you're doing."

"I know what I'm doing," Pace said with unexpected assurance. "And one thing is that I don't believe you. I know Mannering, he wouldn't employ a thug—"

"He employed me all right," Mannering said, "and he wants to know the minute I've got the woman, but don't ask me what he's going to do." He felt a surging impatience, not so much with Pace as with the situation. "Why don't you talk to Mannering—?"

"He isn't going to talk to anybody!" came the voice of Stanley from just behind Pace. "Drop your gun, Pace – and you, whoever you are, drop the woman."

Mannering heard movements behind him, and was sure there was more than one man although no one else spoke. He could just make out the spindly figure of Stanley, clouded in mist. He shifted Lucille's weight and moved his hand towards the pocket where he held the gas pistol, but he did not think he would be able to reach it; and he did not doubt that they would shoot him if they saw what he was doing.

"I won't tell you again," Stanley Peek said in that high-pitched voice; and if the menace in it had been imaginary before, it was real and ominous enough now. "Drop that gun and drop—"

Pace seemed to drop to his knees.

Then, suddenly, he fired at Stanley, the flash from his gun biting through the fog. As he fired he flung himself to the right. Three shots rang out, and one plucked at Mannering's coat, but it was Stanley who staggered, and began to fall. Everything happened at furious speed, blurred by the fog, and uncertainty as to who, and where, everyone was.

Stanley fell sideways, full length.

Pace disappeared into the night.

A man appeared at Mannering's side, and Mannering saw the gun in his hand, felt it poking him in the ribs. At the same time George Peek's voice came from the back doorway, harsh and commanding.

"Take him into the cellar," he ordered. "Take them both down to the cellar."

A man protested: "If the police—"

"If the police heard the shooting, we had a burglar and shot it out," George rasped. "Get them down to the cellar. Make him carry her, for such a knight errant that should be easy enough." He appeared in front of Mannering, and swept his right hand round, the flat of his palm striking Mannering with tremendous force and sending him reeling. "That's just a beginning," he said. "Before I've finished with you you'll wish you'd never been born."

It was the oldest kind of threat; as often as not as empty as the words themselves. But this time it wasn't empty. George meant exactly what he said.

Mannering steadied, and with the gun pointing into his ribs and Lucille over his shoulder he went back into the wash-house. He could not even use their shock, at the discovery that the approach to the steps was open and that the rifle had been fired, to his advantage.

Lucille was too great a burden; with her he had no chance to get away.

19

Second Visit

George Peek demanded. "Did you break in here?" and Mannering said: "Yes." There was no more point in lying.

"If Mannering employs experts like you I wonder what else he gets up to," George said. "When I come again I want to know why he sent you and what you're really after. Maybe if I believe you I'll leave part of you alive."

He went out, covered by the man with the gun, and the steel door began to close.

Mannering did not move until they had been shut off from sight, then he lowered Lucille slowly to a long packing case. He made her as comfortable as he could, judging it would be two hours or more before she came round.

He fingered the temple which had been cut and the cheek which George had struck with such power. He had to think, but first he had to adjust to the fact that he was here, apparently helpless. He had to get used to the idea before he could even begin to think what he could do. And he had to get some facts clear in his mind.

First, that Pace had *not* betrayed his dead partner; and he had escaped.

Second, that if the police had heard the shooting, George Peek would have a thoroughly sound explanation and a wounded Stanley would be all the confirmation needed.

Third, that somewhere on the premises or in the grounds the armed man, or men, had been waiting, and he, or they, were the only positive connection between the Peeks and the attempts to kill him, Mannering.

Fourth: so far he could *prove* no other crime against the Peeks, but Bristow might be able to.

The thoughts passed slowly through his mind, jostling with one another until the most important emerged: the apparent fact that George and his brother knew that the death of old Ezra Peek and of Norman Harcourt had been induced. If he could only prove that . . .

At the moment he would be lucky to stay alive.

He began to move about the cellar, but this time only to examine the walls and ceiling. One thing was immediately evident. This place was as well ventilated as the attic, and that meant a system of ventilation ducts and grills leading above ground.

One of these was in the ceiling at one end of the room; another was high in a corner near the steel door, a third in a corner at the far end of the cellar. And ventilation grills could be made larger; so could ventilation ducts. It would take time, but he would have to try, unless by chance he could find another door. He walked slowly round the cellar, checking the wall between each shelf, one tap at intervals of about eighteen inches. It was a tiring job, and he relaxed for a few minutes, letting thoughts drift through his mind.

What would Pace do, for instance? Would the police come?

These were of course useless speculations, and he started again at the end of the room opposite the door.

Tap-tap-tap-tap. Every place he touched was as solid as rock, and the chance of finding a weak spot grew less and less.

Disheartened, he started at last on the third wall. Every tap which yielded a solid echo brought him nearer to the inevitable: there was no weak spot. This was a cellar deep in the ground, and even if he could get through the concrete, which might be six or seven inches thick, there would be solid earth beyond. If there was a way out it was through one of the ducts or through the door. He examined this with great care, but found nothing in the wall on either side to suggest how to chip through to the electrical supply line; everything was controlled from the outside.

He stared at each of the ventilation bricks in turn, rubbing his eyes. They were getting strained. A glance at his watch told him that it was after midnight, not late but late enough after the day and the night he'd had.

He pulled up a small crate, and sat on it, but it wasn't comfortable.

He would give anything, almost anything, to stretch out for ten or fifteen minutes in comfort.

There was the concrete floor.

Or there was the padded box on which Lucille lay. He looked at her with a crooked smile and then his whole body stiffened, for he thought her eyelids flickered. Tense as he had not been since he had been thrust into this prison he sat and stared at her.

Next time, there was no doubt: her eyes were opening.

Soon after Mannering *alias* Mason had been locked in the cellar, Lorna switched oil television, went into the big room without switching on the lights and looked down into the street. Here the fog was patchy; she could see the ghostly glow about a nearby street lamp but, further away, she could see a light very clearly with little more than a halo about it.

How would the fog affect John?

How long would he be?

And – the question which was always at the back of her mind when he was out on such an expedition – would he come back? It was never possible to calculate the risk that was always there.

The amazing thing was that he could still go out on such a venture without hesitating; as if he did not know the meaning of fear. But he did. In his very early days when she had first known him she had believed that he was insensitive to fear, but now she knew that it was his courage that was undefeatable. He accepted fear, faced it and worked in spite of it. He had so often taken almost desperate chances for other people: sometimes simply because they were human beings in need, sometimes because they had been the victims of some great injustice, never simply for the sake of it.

This time—

Had he really gone because of Lucille?

Would he have ventured out tonight simply because there was some mystery about the Peek Collection? Because two old men might have been killed by some unlawful acceleration of an illness from which they suffered and from which in any case they would soon die?

Or had he gone because he was in love with Lucille?

That was the first time she had used the phrase 'in love with' and it made her wince a little, but she could also smile at herself. There wasn't room for her jealousy. There might be no way of avoiding it, but it could do no good. And she had thought herself almost proof against it. A few years ago each of them had felt the strong pull of an illicit attraction; she did not know whether John knew she had, for a while, had a lover; she did not know whether he had ever had a mistress but she did know that for a while the strain between them had been so great that the bonds of marriage had nearly snapped.

But they endured, and in many ways become stronger than ever; or she had thought they had until the advent of Lucille.

She could remember laughing as he had told her how the two of them had cannoned into each other. Normally, after such an encounter, they would have sprung apart, but she guessed, she *knew* that instead, his arms had gone protectively about Lucille and for a moment they had looked – perhaps felt – like lovers. Very soon afterwards Lorna noticed that her husband had been more preoccupied than usual. Several times she had seen Lucille, and had wondered, then, whether they were in the middle of an *affaire.* If they were, Lucille could hardly have been more indiscreet.

Now she knew they had not been; but she was not sure that the situation was not worse, for obviously John was fighting against a surge of emotion which could engulf him. One part of her longed to cry out: go with her, take her, let it burn itself out, and the other part of her longed for assurance that it was only a passing interest, not even serious enough to smoulder.

The telephone bell rang.

She thought: John! and sprang up, forgetting her ankle, wincing when she put her full weight on it and dropping into a chair by the telephone in the study.

"Mrs. Mannering," she said, and held her breath in the hope of hearing his voice.

"I'd like to speak to Mr. Mannering," a man said. There was something in his voice which told her that this certainly was not an ordinary social call. "Urgently, please."

"I'm sorry, but my husband isn't here."

After a moment's pause the man muttered in a despairing voice: "Oh, my God," and he was obviously so distressed that he filled her with alarm. "When—when will he be back?"

"I'm not sure, but perhaps I can help," Lorna said, urgently. "I know most—"

"I *must* talk to him." The man's voice was filled with despair.

"I may be able to help," Lorna said. "I am in his confidence." She just prevented herself from asking who he was for the question might scare him away. "I think he is looking for a Mrs. Peek—"

"You know about Lucille?"

"I really am in his confidence." Lorna made herself sound so much calmer than she felt. "And if you will tell me what you want I may be able to help. He left me certain instructions." That was no more than half true but it might help.

"I can't tell you who I am," the man said, obviously lighting to control his agitation, "but this I can say. I've just shot a man named Stanley Peek, I was at the Peeks' house. I saw a man there who said he worked for Mr. Mannering."

John, breathed Lorna.

"He was carrying Lucille Peek, and she seemed unconscious," the man went on. "There was shooting and I got away, but I know this man was taken prisoner, with Lucille—"

"Was he hurt?" Lorna still contrived to keep her voice steady.

"I don't know for certain but I don't think so. The house is in Ealing, 24 Cirencester Street. I wanted to tell Mr. Mannering that this other man and Lucille Peek were there. I couldn't stay and help, it—it would have been impossible, there were five or six men in the grounds. Will you—will you be able to do anything?"

"I can try," Lorna said in a bleak voice. "Please get off the line."

She called Bristow and told him exactly what the caller had said; she did not need to add that Bristow was fully aware that the 'man who worked for Mannering' was Mannering himself. In a mood close to despair she wondered what Bristow could possibly do, what she could do. Bristow's voice cut across her thoughts, sharp and incisive.

"Hold tight, Lorna. I shall call the Yard and tell them I believe Lucille is being kept at the Peeks' house against her will and that there's been shooting in the grounds. Even if it hasn't been reported I think they'll send a search party. If they do find Lucille it will be half the battle. If they found John as his *alter ego* it will be up to him to get out of trouble. Better have to greet the police than the Peeks. Do you agree?"

"Yes," Lorna said. "Yes." But she thought frantically that in one way it might conceivably be worse. For how would he explain his presence at the house, and in disguise?

Chief Superintendent Gordon of New Scotland Yard was on duty when Bristow telephoned. At one time one of Bristow's Chief Assistants, now the Yard's specialist on precious stones, there had been a time when he had been bitterly hostile to Mannering. But those days were past, and he listened intently and responded without hesitation.

"All right, Bill. I'll talk to Ealing and I'll send some of our men along, too. Why don't we meet you there?"

About the same time as this, George Peek was looking at his brother, who was sitting up in bed, his left arm and shoulder heavily bandaged. The doctor who had come to dress the wound had left, and now Stanley looked pale but relaxed in spite of an underlying tension which affected the two of them.

"One day we'll get Pace," he said, "but there's no need to worry about him now. What we have to worry about are the police."

"If they come, we'll do what I said before," replied George. "We caught a burglar and he shot his way out. We've sealed off the washroom; no one is going to find the cellar."

"Mannering's man did," Stanley put in thinly.

"That must have been a fluke. We've taken the gun away from downstairs—"

"George," Stanley interrupted, "it wouldn't matter if you had a hundred guns rigged up downstairs *provided the police don't find the cellar.* If they do we're done for. If they don't we'll be O.K. once Lucille's mouth is shut forever, and the man's as well. And Mannering's, he probably guesses too much already."

George said heavily: "Mannering's one thing, the two downstairs another. They can rot to death. I tell you we don't need to worry. All the police will find is you in bed with a bullet wound, and me with a bruise on my chest where that swine kicked me – there's the evidence. I've sent the boys home, they'll stay put until we want them again. There's nothing to worry about provided you don't panic."

He stopped speaking and for a few moments there was silence; a silence broken abruptly by the ringing of the front door bell, heavy banging on the knocker and, from outside, the wailing of a police siren.

"I'll go and let them in," George said. He got up hurriedly and made for the stairs. The manservant was already at the door, wearing a dressing-gown over his pyjamas, and all George Peek had to do was pull back the top bolt.

Four policemen stood outside on the porch.

There were four more on the drive, still more at the back, all of them vague and misty figures in the fog. George complained bitterly about how long they had been in coming, lied smoothly when claiming that he had sent for them soon after the shooting, told the carefully prepared story he and his brother had rehearsed.

The police searched every room, all the outhouses including the old-fashioned wash-house, the garages, every place they could find. Neither of the Peeks questioned Bristow's presence, both appeared to give all the help they could.

Absolutely nothing was found.

"Absolutely nothing was found," Bristow said to Lorna, at the Chelsea flat. "It looks to me as if John worked one of his miracles, and got away with Lucille. You might hear from him at any time. But just in case of new developments Gordon left two men in the grounds, with orders to keep a lookout, and to make another search in the morning. Not that they'll be able to, unless the fog clears," he added gruffly. "It's like an old-fashioned pea-souper outside. Mind if I use your spare room?"

What he really meant was that he did not want to leave Lorna here alone for the night: and he was as anxious as she to know the moment John telephoned.

If he telephoned.

Mannering lay on the long crate, with Lucille by his side. She was asleep, but it was a natural sleep now, and it would not take much to wake her. All but one light was out, and that was behind them, so there was no strain on their eyes. Physically more relaxed, he had time to go over and over again the whole affair from his very first encounter with Lucille.

It was strange, to feel so close and yet be aware of no desire.

Perhaps it was the pressures of the day. Perhaps he was just physically exhausted. Perhaps some change had taken place in him, emotionally. Whatever the cause, her beauty, her desirability, left him untouched, his heart growing heavier with every moment. It was two o'clock, his wristwatch said. The police were certainly not coming tonight.

But the police had come, and gone.

20

Way Out?

There *must* be a way out.

He had been locked into strong-rooms before, and found some outlet; he had been in prisons, and escaped. He had run the gauntlet of a hundred policemen in the same building searching for him, and they had not caught him. He had been in foul and evil-smelling dungeons, and was a free man – until today. There *must* be a way out.

He felt Lucille move, and knew that she had woken. He felt her body stir, and saw her turn her head. There was enough light for her to take in the shelves and their contents, for her to know where she was. Suddenly she saw Mannering and gave a convulsive start.

"It's all right," he said. "No need to be scared."

It was not until he spoke that she realised who he was. She stared, holding her breath. Awareness had come too soon after waking; she began to shiver. For the first time he put his arm about her.

She gulped, and moistened her lips.

"We—we are in the cellar."

"Yes."

"In the cellar," she repeated in a tone as of horror.

"Lucille," he said, "do you know a way out – except by the main door?"

Those golden-coloured eyes looked frantically into his; and her breathing grew uneven.

"There is no way," she said. "Oh, John, why did you come here?"

"I came to find out what was happening," he said. "And I have found out."

"If you had stayed away—"

"You would still have been a prisoner here."

"I am not important," she said, impatiently. "I did not want to ruin—" She broke off and closed her eyes; and it was like the turning off of a light. Her voice was dull and despairing as she repeated: "There is no other way out."

"There has to be," he said.

She did not speak but moistened her lips again, and he realised that she must be parched. He must get her some water. He eased himself away from her and went to the little cloakroom, ran a paper cup of cold water and as he ran the tap and turned it off there was a rattling of sound in the pipes. An air-lock, perhaps—

"My God!" he breathed.

He carried the water back to her, then pulled a smaller crate immediately beneath the ceiling ventilation shaft. The grill itself was easy to take off now that he had loosened it. There was little or no dust about the edges. He could see only a few inches inside, not far enough to discern what the sides of the airduct were made of. Metal, porcelain or brick? He tapped with the nails of his right hand. A little tinny echo returned to him. He tried more sharply with a bent finger, and now there was a kind of boom.

Lucille called: "John!"

He thought: Not now, not now! Here was a way of getting a message up to the surface, and this must surely lead to an open space in the garden.

"John, take this!"

This? He glanced down impatiently, saw that she was handing him a sheathed knife: metal! He took it and tapped several times and the sound was clear and loud – but could it be heard above ground? And if it were, who would hear it? George or Stanley

Peek, or their men, or—

He changed the beat to the S.O.S. signal, so easy to make and familiar to millions – if there was only one of those millions to hear it.

S.O.S.

He kept on slowly and deliberately until his arm was too tired to continue. Then Lucille took over.

Two policemen on duty in the grounds heard the tapping but were not sure what it was.

George Peek, sleeping in a room close to the ventilation grid, heard it first in his sleep, and then gradually into his consciousness.

S.O.S.

For a few minutes he lay in bed, recognising the sound without immediately identifying it, but gradually it impinged itself on his mind.

S.O.S.

"My God!" he rasped, and pushed the bedclothes back and went to the window. Here it was, a clear and unmistakable sound, for the shaft was immediately below the window and a drainpipe seemed to pick it up and magnify it.

S.O.S. S.O.S.

He pulled on trousers and a top coat over his pyjamas and slipped down the stairs and out the back way. The noise was still unmistakable, but not so loud here – although loud enough. He went straight to the garages and opened the middle one, got into the wheel of a Jaguar and started the engine. He backed out slowly, knowing exactly what he had to do, sure that it could not fail. He reversed until the exhaust pipe was just above the ventilation grille so that the exhaust fumes struck the wall of the house and were thrown back beneath the car and into the grille and the duct. The engine idled quietly. The stink of the exhaust was bad even ten yards from the car. George Peek moved away.

It was too cold to stay out, and he had no idea how long it would take the carbon-monoxide to take effect in the cellar. The fumes would be too strong in his own room for him to go back to bed but there was a small room across the courtyard where he could hear the beat of the engine, and through it the interminable tap-tap-tap-tap of the call for help. He reached the room and opened the window a fraction. Both sounds were quite audible.

"Half-an-hour ought to be enough," he said to himself, and he sat in an armchair and put his feet up on a smaller chair, with the light full on. Whatever happened, he mustn't go to sleep.

Mannering was the first to smell the exhaust fumes, for they began during one of his periods of tapping out the message, but within a few minutes Lucille, too, was just as acutely aware of what was happening. She looked up at him, her face drawn and white.

"How long will it take, John?"

"There's no way of telling. George or Stanley must have heard us – so someone else might."

"It is no use to lie to ourselves," Lucille said, with the unnatural calmness of one prepared to die, "I am only sorry that I involved you in this." She watched as he continued to tap, and then went on: "But this I can tell you. My husband planned this fraud before he died: but he had no intention of sharing it with his sons. I am desolated because his hatred of them stemmed from their hatred of me."

She broke off, coughing. And Mannering, too, began to cough, fighting to check himself, knowing that it could so easily grow into a paroxysm which he could not stop.

Lucille went on, her voice growing hoarse and uncertain: "I believe they killed him because of it, and I believe they killed Mr. Harcourt because Stanley told him. And they tried to prevent me from telling you and tried to kill you after you had been to my flat, in case I had told you. They have always had men who worked for them, hired thieves and killers, desperate men whom they paid well. They live in a small house near here and come whenever they are wanted, willing to do whatever they are told."

Mannering began to cough again, and for a moment paused in his tapping.

"John," Lucille said, "it is not worth going on." She clung to him. "I wanted the real Collection, they wanted me to have the fake one, and wanted me to sell it. I had your valuation, on such a word as yours every buyer would be satisfied. And I must tell you I would have agreed if I had not fallen in love with you.

"All those other reasons I gave you were false, John.

"My husband was a criminal, I also am one – but he and I, we were not murderers. We—"

There was a sudden cessation in the throbbing of the engine; there was another sound, the sharp crack of a shot. Yet a third – a man's voice coming along the duct towards them.

"Hallo, down there, can you hear me? . . . Can you hear me?"

Mannering said hoarsely: "Loud and clear. Who are you?"

"We are police officers. Do you know where you are and how we can reach you?"

"Yes," Mannering gasped between fits of coughing. "There is an—old wash-house at the back, and—the metal boiler moves if you press both the On and the Off switch together. Beneath—it are the cellar—steps."

"We'll be down in two shakes," the man called. "Just hold on."

Mannering turned very slowly away from the ventilation hole. 'Two shakes' might mean ten or fifteen minutes but it did not matter now, they would be rescued in time.

Away from the ventilation hole, the air was better and he could speak more easily.

"Lucille," he said, "no one need know that you worked on criminal acts with your husband. The sons might try to involve you but a good counsel could almost certainly get you off."

"But John Mannering knows," she said. "The one honest man." There was actually a gleam of laughter in her eyes.

"And you know that tonight John Mannering was someone else," he said. "Shall we make a bargain? If you don't tell the police who I am, I won't tell them what you've told me."

She drew back, as if astounded. "*You,* afraid of the police!"

"No," he answered, "but there are some things I'd prefer them not to know."

"So," she said. "John – afterwards, will you—will you sell the Collection for me?"

"*Was* it stolen?"

"No, that was what I told you to hide the truth. The idea was to switch the real for the false."

"I will sell them for you," he promised, and quite suddenly he held out his arms and she moved towards him, into them. He held her very tightly but did not kiss her, and she did not turn her face up towards him. They seemed to stay like that for a long time.

"To one side of John Mannering, goodbye," she said with forced lightness. "John, it would be so good if we—if you and Lorna and I could be friends."

As she spoke there was a click of sound, and almost at once the steel door began to slide open. Four policemen appeared . . .

Fifteen minutes later, after knowing that George Peek had been charged with attempted murder by carbon-monoxide poisoning and had been taken away, Mannering allowed himself to be led towards a police car. He had given his name as Mason, with a fictitious address. He was not under charge, there was concern for him but no need to keep a close watch.

One moment he was there, tall and powerful-looking, in the fog.

The next he had disappeared.

Lorna was still awake, but in bed, when Mannering came down from the attic, after entering from the house next door and crossing the roof, there removing his disguise.

"John," Lorna said, "Oh my darling. Thank God that you're really safe."

"I'm safe enough," Mannering said heavily.

"And Lucille?"

"If I've any doubts left about Lucille it's that she *was* the only person present at the last seizures of both Ezra Peek and Norman Harcourt."

"No she wasn't," said Bristow, his voice wafting calmly from the spare room. "One of the things I learned tonight was the name of the Peeks' doctor. He's been the family doctor for a long time. His name is Medway, and he has offices in Ealing and lives in Wimbledon."

"Harcourt's doctor!" cried Mannering. "Bill," he added urgently, "make sure he's closely questioned in the morning. He—"

"He's being closely questioned now," Bristow said calmly. "And I don't think there'll be much difficulty in proving that he gave both Peek and Harcourt overdoses of digitalis by injection. Do you remember an elderly man and his daughter at Harcourt's office?"

"Good Lord! Was that Medway?"

"Complete with whiskers and a wig," said Bristow, and added drily: "It's amazing what can be done with disguises these days, isn't it?"

Mannering chuckled.

Nothing more was said, as Bristow, with a gigantic yawn which could be clearly heard, went back to sleep.

It was Bristow who called from Quinn's next morning to report that Dr. Medway had been charged with conspiracy to murder both Ezra Peek and Norman Harcourt; he had accused the Peek brothers of blackmailing him into doing what they wanted because for years he had bought stolen objets d'art from them. The brothers had accused Lucille of complicity but no charge had been made.

"Young Pace of Harcourt, Pace and Pace is going to defend her," Bristow said. "And from what I can gather, with a lot of fervour. I don't know whether this is the time to tell you, John, that he's been a widower for the past two years . . ."

"I always had a feeling he was a dark horse," Mannering murmured.

In fact the one thing he wanted to know was why Pace had been at the house the previous night. As Mannering he did not know Pace had been there, but there was no reason why 'Mason' should not have recognised him. Mannering decided to repress his curiosity; Pace might well put two and two together, even if Lucille did not confide in him.

"John," Lucille said on the telephone a few days later, "I can now tell you that Charles Pace also is a good man, and brave as well. He did not believe his partner's death was natural, he did not trust Dr. Medway, and he knew about my husband's criminal past because Mr. Harcourt had told him. So, Charles pretended to work for George and for Stanley. He returned because he believed you and I were at the house. He is a little puzzled because he found another man carrying me. It would not be wise for me to tell him who that other man really was, would it?"

"It would put too great a burden on his curiosity, and perhaps later on his conscience."

"Now that is something I would not like," declared Lucille. "My lips, they are sealed."

And when Mannering told her of this, Lorna said: And do you know I really believe they are." There was a long pause before she went on brightly: "Darling, while you were out the hospital called. Josh is going to be all right, and he may have visitors. And while we're there we must see the young man who saved him. He's got *seven* fractures . . ."

The young man with the seven fractures lay in a hospital bed with his legs in plaster casts. He was surprisingly cheerful for one who had suffered so much injury. Perhaps Lorna, and Josh, and Mannering, had something to do with it.

Three months later he was an assistant at Quinn's.

JOHN CREASEY

GIDEON'S DAY

Gideon's day is a busy one. He balances family commitments with solving a series of seemingly unrelated crimes from which a plot nonetheless evolves and a mystery is solved.

One of the most senior officers within Scotland Yard, George Gideon's crime solving abilities are in the finest traditions of London's world famous police headquarters. His analytical brain and sense of fairness is respected by colleagues and villains alike.

'The finest of all Scotland Yard series' – New York Times.

GIDEON'S FIRE

Commander George Gideon of Scotland Yard has to deal successively with news of a mass murderer, a depraved maniac, and the deaths of a family in an arson attack on an old building south of the river. This leaves little time for the crisis developing at home ....

'Gideon of Scotland Yard emerges as one of the most real working detectives in modern fiction.... A sympathetic and believable professional policeman.' - New York Times

JOHN CREASEY

THE CREEPERS

"The prisoner's hand was thin and bony ... And in the centre of the palm was a pinkish mark. It was the shape of a wolf's head, mouth open, fangs showing. Although it was what he had expected to see, Inspector West felt a twinge of repugnance a stab not unrelated to fear. It was the fifth time he had seen the mark of the wolf – the mark of Lobo."

A gang of cat burglars led by Lobo cause mayhem as they terrorize the city. They must be stopped, but with little in the way of evidence the police are baffled. Just how can Inspector West manage to do this in what is a race against time before more victims succumb?

"Here is an excellent novel of law enforcement officers, harried, discouraged and desperately fatigued, moving inexorably ahead under the pressure of knowledge that they must succeed to save human lives." - Cleveland Plain-Dealer

"Furiously exciting" - Chicago Tribune

"The action is fast, continuous and exciting" - San Francisco News

JOHN CREASEY

THE HOUSE OF THE BEARS

Standing alone in the bleak Yorkshire Moors is Sir Rufus Marne's 'House of the Bears'. Dr. Palfrey is asked to journey there to examine an invalid - who has now disappeared. Moreover, Marne's daughter lies terribly injured after a fall from the minstrel's gallery which Dr. Palfrey discovers was no accident. He sets out to investigate and the results surprise even him . . . .

"'Palfrey' and his boys deserve to take their places among the immortals." - Western Mail

INTRODUCING THE TOFF

Whilst returning home from a cricket match at his father's country home, the Honourable Richard Rollison - alias The Toff - comes across an accident which proves to be a mystery. As he delves deeper into the matter with his usual perseverance and thoroughness , murder and suspense form the backdrop to a fast moving and exciting adventure.

'The Toff has been promoted to a place of honour among amateur detectives.' – The Times Literary Supplement